Flight to Finland:

A Noveramatry

A combination of novel, drama and poetry all in one line
on the issue of immigration that every Finn and
immigrant residing in Finland should read

Affectionately dedicated to

UUU
U
U
UUU

who believe there is no skin between us

Mehdi Ghasemi

Flight to Finland:

A Noveramatry

**A combination of novel, drama and poetry all in one line
on the issue of immigration that every Finn and
immigrant residing in Finland should read**

Front Cover Photo: Mehdi Ghasemi
Cover and Interior Design: Mehdi Ghasemi

Publisher: BoD™ – Books on Demand, Helsinki, Finland

Manufacturer: Books on Demand GmbH, Norderstedt, Germany

ISBN: 978-952-339-384-4

Con10ts

10. Season Four:

Traveler in the White Dark

Learned Custos, Esteemed Opponent, Ladies and Gentlemen,
As the first African American playwright who received Pulitzer Prize for drama, Charles Gordone devoted major parts of his professional life to the pursuit of multi-racial affinity and unity. Gordone's plays also challenge the racist, classist and sexist stereotypes ascribed to African American men and women. This can be seen in the at10tion he pays to the intersectional issue of race, class and gender inequality. Oh my God! I'm defending my doctoral dissertation! Thank you Finland! Intersectionality holds that various biological, economic, cultural, political and social categories such as race, class, gender, sexual orientations and other axes of identity interact, creating a system of oppression that reflects the intersection of multiple forms of domination or discrimination. How far I've come! This journey is also coming to an end. I have only some more hours to go. The relationships among these various axes are like a mathematical equation, in which each axis has a single, direct but additive effect on the equation. It is worth noting that intersectionality is a concept of10 used in critical theories to describe the ways in which over-

lapping oppressions are interconnected to debase a person or a community; however, it can also apply to the intersecting orientations and institutions that interrelate to grant privilege to a person or a community. Intersectionality of persis10ce, determination and hard work plus commitment, expertise and experience of my supervisors plus my family's support here and there made this possible.

Just a question before I proceed with my lectio. While writing this noveramatry, several titles came to my mind: Flight to Fineland, Flight to Funland, Flight to Finland, Flight to Fundland and Flight to Fanland, and eventually I went for the one right in the middle! Which one would you choose if you were in my shoes? Please underline it.

In my dissertation, I approach a number of Gordone's plays from the perspectives of intersectionality. I remember the first day I started. So cold it was, 'scold and right from the first day I learned that I have to fend against harshness. I draw upon the ways Gordone uses to challenge the dominant hierarchal systems in which whites hold hegemonic power and accordingly predominate in roles of political and social leadership and economic control to which I refer as "whitestream." The by-passers all looked down and watched their steps. Oli tosi liukas.[1] I show how his plays lend themselves to a range of intersecting theories to utter the concerns of African Americans and release them from the dominant ideologies that have entangled them throughout histo-

2

ry. A moment of looking up was enough to change your position from vertical to horizontal.

Five years passed since that slippery day, five years of hard work, five years full of memories, sweet and sad. I remember the first day we got on a bus in Finland. We knew nowhere and nowhere knew us. Two old ladies sitting behind us were talking in Finnish. I lis10ed carefully and this was what I heard: yo yo misteman suoamalistonut lasudenessa vartaradiossa arkaises aikaseminehka golla yoo yoo mukaan me gerra queen aikasemin puurakenteine torile samma miks voivoi palyoon tulossa loppu soravame olkomalaikiyainen noni vieraspaikkakuntalainen yoo yoo gadso gire verotosi tale balyonkun dulen ya sa lopoo kun kosgematoni illiman mutta koko sooks valateksia ya gireteinpain yoyo ostavanraha lassikoondele heivan yos me veroayorata.[2] Igotbutnothingandjustthere ymmärsin, että suomen kieli ei ole vaikkeaa, ja jos menet suomen kielen kurssille 24/7 noin vain 10 vuotta, voit varmasti oppia ja puhua sen kuin robotti.[3]

In his play *No Place to Be Somebody*, Gordone writes the story of a black bar10der named Johnny Romero who tries to interpret his piece of the American Dream in a New York City neighborhood where most venues are run by white mafia. Pete Zerroni who leads the white mafia disapproves of blacks in his territory and he burns down their places. Under such harsh circumstances, Johnny and a number of denizens of his bar still work and wait for the fulfilment of their dreams which turn to be an illusion or rather a delusion. My dream to see this day but how would be life after PhD? Miten menee?[4] Indeterminacy kills but indeterminacy is the beauty of life. Fixity kills. Johnny's best friend named Gabe Gabriel is an unemployable mulatto actor. This is my BIG day after all. May 10 may be as memorable as my birthday. It may be another scarlet day in my calendar. Gabe is cast neither as a white man, since he is too dark for white roles, nor as a black man, since he is too light for black ones. Due to this problem, he resorts to writing and performing his own plays. Five years of determination is coming to an end, five perspiratory years will be coming to an end, five years of diligence came to an end. I have come to defend with a very sharp pen which is mightier than the sword, a strong black suit made of good fabrics and a bottle of orange juice "100% natural, without preservatives, artificial colors, flavors or added sugars." Gabe addresses his audiences directly and speaks of his own problems which self-reflexively and self-reflectively reveal both the artifice and artificiality of his plays.

I now respectfully beg my esteemed opponent appointed by the Faculty of Humanities to present his criticisms of my doctoral dissertation.

This disse'tation, entitled *Postrace Drama: A Study of Selected Plays by Cha'les Go'done*, offe's a series of relevant readi'gs of selected plays by Cha'les Go'done. It shows ability to car'y out independent schola'ly wo'k as requi'ed from a doctoral disse'tation. The thesis shows a good knowledge of the prima'y texts studied and the litera'y criticism dealing with them.

What is next? How would be life after PhD? A BIG suspense. In some countries cloud seeding is quite prevalent. Cloud seeding is a form of weather modification to increase the amount of precipitation, either rain or snow, that falls from clouds by dispersing substances into the air that serve as cloud condensation. This phenomenon alters the microphysical processes within the cloud. To put it simply, in some countries, especially with dry climates, water is scarce but it is possible to artificially create rainfall through cloud seeding which is very expensive and requires a very exact calculation. Thus, a country may spend a lot of time, budget and energy on this project but as a result of miscalculation, the seeded clouds might move to a different country and rain there. As far as I know, some of the ceded clouds that have been seeded here are raining somewhere else and some more are packing. My husband almost every month mentions the name of a ceded cloud that is packing and heading for some other countries. Cloud ceding does not just happen between countries. It might even happen between universities and even departments.

What comes next? I have always faced this type of indeterminacy in my life. I clearly remember the few months' time before our Flight to Finland. We had received our visas but still were uncertain to buy tickets. Months of stress we had. We really didn't know what is are was were will be waiting for us. What types of

5

people we meet? What the hand of destiny has writ10 for us?
What has fate prepared for us? This is the poem I wrote at those
critical moments:

Indeterminacy

Indeterminacy kills us

Curiosity kills the cats

But wee've been born to die

As ephemeral arts do!

Any way not to die?

Confusion kills us

Double voicedness in head, twoness

Two or too?

You speak while silent

Your silence is heavy and light

Your speech smooth and harsh

I hesitant, you confused

Perhaps wee stay alive

if you stop and give me five

A hi five

Are you sure five *is are* enuf?

Which one? Is or are?

Are you sure?

Shall wee go?

Shall wee no?

Wee'll die if we're sure

But what four?

Four or for?

Incredulity kills us

Curiosity kills the rats

Confusion keeps us killed

Indeterminacy kills all!

Yestertodaymorrow I was am being in swimming pool, floating and thinking how to proceed with my story: To open all valves of my heart to you and tell you all sʇɔɐɟ sweet and sad or to say some selected sweet sections. Someone just arced into pool, ejecting water out of pool and onto my face. I lost my balance and just there I decided to tell you all sʇɔɐɟ, mainly because as far as I know wise people admit that no one is perfect and thus they love to be aware of ʇɔɐɟ complements rather than mere fake compliments and this is the secret behind their progress.

We arrived in Helsinki after lots of challenges. Due to mist, our transit flight at Vienna airport was cancelled and we had to re-book another flight to Helsinki which happened in about 10 hours. My kid fell seriously ill. Worriedly and hurriedly, we found a small clinic at Vienna airport. Doctor visited her and di-agnosed that tiredness is the main reason, believing that carrot soup would help her recover. "But where can I find carrot soup?" The doctor had no idea! Any carrot soup tablet or capsule invented? The doctor gave me a bill and I had to pay 40 euros. That made me sick as well ☺ The transit flight was near. I searched uphill and down dale and found no soup. I felt dizzy and my head was muzzy. I wished the doctor himself had made and sold carrot soup and I was willing to pay 40 more euros for a bowl of carrot soup on those critical moments.

I had have had a caring friend in Helsinki but unfortunately he was out of Finland when we alived. That made our situation tougher. We headed for office of house agency from which we had rented a house, showed our documents, signed the lease, received the keys and found our way towards the house with difficulty. Everywhere was white and pavements had been covered by ice and we had to watch every step of ours. We entered the house. It was full of nothing not even light bulbs. We knew nowhere and nowhere knew us. Where are we now? Just knew that we are somewhere in the north of the globe. Before we open our luggage, it got dark, extremely dark, and we passed the darkest night ever in our life. To skip darkness, we decided to go to bed early, the bed which was not there. We had to make it with whatever we had in our luggage. A very tough night we passed.

Let's sta't with this question: can we say that in Go'done's plays, pa'ticula'ly in *No Place to Be Somebody* and *Little Mo' Light Around the Place*, the present pushes us into the past to reconfigu'e the futu'e? I mean to refigu' the past racial mispe'ceptions of African Americans in orde' to prefigu' postblackness?

Yes. Gordone distorts the borderlines between past present and future 10ses. As a result, the reconfiguration of the past emerges in the present and immediately the reconfiguration of the present manifests itself in the past. I interpret this to mean that there would be no difference between past present and future if African Americans fail to reconfigure their prospects resulting in no improvement in their status and their racial representations and as a result discrimination, injustice and inequality against them will continue in the future. At the same time, Godone represents different types of black people showing them in different positions with different mentalities in order to show the diversity of black people, the diversity of their ideologies, visions and practices, the diversity of their approaches to face the challenges, the diversity of black identities, and this helps Gordone to challenge the old conception of Blackness, to offer new perspectives for not-same-old Blackness and to question the reign of a single notion of Blackness. So postblackness in these plays does not mean that we are over Blackness but we are over a single definition of what Blackness means.

I suppose this is true about immigrants. So we can propose the idea of "Postemigration." Let me return to my own chronicle. Early morn, I walked out in seek of a shop to do some shopping with carrot soup ingredients on top of my list. The nearest I found was about half an hour walk. It was so cold. Later I found it was -25°C. The worse part was the time that I did some shopping and was on my way back home with my hands out holding two full heavy plastic bags. I alived home but felt like a snowman. Even my eyelashes and nostrils were frozen. I was afraid to touch any member of my body thinking they are fragile and might b-reak. It took me 10 minutes to find my five senses back, forget about the sixth one!

We had some breakfast and made some soup for my kid. Having heard from Finland consul in my home country that aliens have to visit a police station and register their entrance upon their arrival, we planned to visit police station later that day. We waited in bus stop for about 3×10 minutes and no bus showed up. Some other passengers who were standing next to us were also shivering. I was worried about my kid who had not thoroughly recovered. Please close your eyes and imagine you are in a bus stop waiting for about 3×10 minutes in -25°C. No one complained and some years later we found that it is against sisu[5] to complain! No matter what happens, you should bear and grin it! And I still do not understand if people always bear and grin it, how those in charge will learn about their defects and remove them? Sometimes complaint is a must. Complaint does not necessarily signify a belligerent attitude; it can be through a friendly notification or a clement petition. If we always bear and grin it, how my colleague who attends workplace every day with her high-heeled shoes and steps extremely loudly on the office wooden floors all day long learns that we are really annoyed? Eventually, a bus arrived and no one asked why the previous bus did not show up!

Upon getting on the bus, I asked driver whether he passes by police station or somewhere nearby and she nodded. Then we asked him to kindly inform us when we arrive. She nodded again. We sat behind her so that he couldn't forget us. After about 10 minutes she looked at us and just pointed outside and we thought he means we have to get off and we did. Then we looked everywhere in search of police station but failed to find any. My husband asked a by-passer and she told us to go straight. Hopefully we get there soon, we thought. We walked for about 10 minutes but did not find it. Asked another passer-by desperately and he said we have to follow our frozen noses ---------------------------. I could not move my hands any more. To protect ourselves from cold, every now and then we went into some shops on our way, and to make our visits look natural, I sometimes looked at prices which increased my blood pressure and helped me warm up. We also found a second-hand shop on the way to police station. I cast a glance and found that a chair costs 200 euros! Some small simple chandelier was about 300 euros and I thought I need at least 3 of them to partially light our rented home! O my goodness! How can we survive here? My forehead and face got covered in sweat. I blamed myself. I asked my wife to quit her nice job and accompany me. She trusted me. I was drowned in these thoughts when one word in a label on a table did catch my eye: "antiikki." O my God! We are in an antique shop and not in a second-hand one.

We finally found and alived the police station. We got in. I got a number with my numb hand. It was warm and we didn't want to leave there till summer. We started melting but my kid's coughs which happened every now and again made us worried. Waited for about 10 minutes. It was our turn. "You are in a wrong place?" police officer advised us. "You should go to Maistraatti.[6]" My temp rose! "But where is Maistraatti?" "It's down this street, about a 10 minute walk." Another maze! As soon as we got out, my wife clearly said that she won't stay in this country for even a second. She was determined to return to our home country. I talked to her for a while so as to soothe her. "Just give me a few days' time and I'll make a cozy life for you." But I myself was not sure about my promise. I don't know where to go and what to do. I do not know even one person in this town. I have no one here. I'm an alien. A gnikcuf A —.—

9. Finnagain Wake

A Play in Four Panels

List of Figments:

The Finnish Finn

The Swedish Finn

The First Woman Voter

The First Finnish Immigrant

The Veteran

The Police Wo-Man

The Emigrant

The Finnish Refugee

The Meta-Medium

The Gabe Gabriel

King Charles Frederick

The Chorus

The Setting: Whenever and wherever you wish. For example,

Place: Here

Time: The present of the past

8. Panel One:

A Man who Walked Naked

The First Finnish Immigrant
Did you hear what The Emigrant said? It's always hard for new arrivals. I fully understand them. I have been an immigrant myself.

The Finnish Refugee
I understand them, too. I've been myself in such critical condisions [sic]. But in my time, evacuee families who were forced to leave their homes were warmly embraced by other Finnis families.

The Veteran
Do you remember the economic depresion during the wars? Do you? Muistatteko, että[7] food and other goods were in sort [sic] supply?

The First Finnish Voter
It's really hard to understand some people until you see things from their perspectives.

The Finnish Finn
How can we forget? We made shoes out of paper and wood.

The Swedish Finn
We also made kaffe substitute from dandelion roots.

The Emigrant
I remember once when it was silent, I could clearly hear a dandelion florets talking together. One of them was saying, "Soon it's time for me to fly. I will get rid of stagnancy, I mean sitting here all the time. I fly graciously. The sun will shine on me and wind

makes me dance and sing. What a . . . ." The other floret inter-rupted her company, "I will go so far far far away. I'll land on a fineland, plant myself and root. It would be a new life for me and my descendants. I beautify that land and my next generations will make that land finer and finer. Another florent was totally pessimistic: "These are forlorn hopes, I suppose. You might fly all these long middle passages in search of your dreams but when you get there, it's cold and probably a bit late to root, the frozen soil might reject you so you will die out. The fourth one that was following this conversation at10tively opened his mouth: "So you mean there is no point in moving?" she asked hesitantly. "But it would be ridiculous not to move, we are born to move, and without movement we die too," the other objected. Then there happened a very long and noisy argument among them. I could not clearly hear what they say and thus I left.

The Meta-Medium
The brea-king news. Scientists have found in their recent studies that the yellow ants and black ones repel each other. In their ex-periments, they moved a black ant from his nest and located him in front of the yellow ants' nest. They observed that yellow ants took distance from the black one and even to avoid him they changed their ways. Scientists are hopeful to apply this finding to the redefinition of postethnicity, ingroup and outgroup relations.

The Swedish Finn
This discourse is familjär. It sounds like Voice On Thuh Tee V.

The Emigrant
You said it.

The Gabe Gabriel
Aint dat nice. Scientists hav' worked dis- much tuh question multi-racial affinity? Not promisin' huh?

The Finnish Finn
For whom?

16

The Emigrant
I need only justice, just this and not dis-. Is that a big demand?

The Meta-Medium
Another brea-king news. The recent research conducted by Institute of Human Becoming shows that Finns are reserved. The research also shows that communication is more required in heterogeneous multicultural societies wherein different cultures mingle. The research reveals that in such societies people have different backgrounds, worldviews and experiences, and communication makes people aware of those differences.

The Finnish Finn
Reserved!? Hahaha but minä puhun paljon[8] in this play.

The Veteran
I speak enaf but I prefer not to inisiate conversasion. You just have to make the first move and see what I do. I need some warm up.

The First Finnish Immigrant
I first settled down in Ashtabala Harbor. I worked hard day and night, ate less and saved more so that I could send tickets to my wife and two of my children, just two of them. The other two stayed behind in Finland with their grandparents. We worked hard and saved some more money to send them two more tickets. It took some years before my kids could join us but to our surprise they were no longer kids. They were teenagers. Ididnotrecognizethemwhentheyarrived but the rate of mortality was high for youngers and I lost two of them.

The Finnish Finn & The Swedish Finn
You are history.

The Emigrant
National generalization is always unfair. To me Finns are neither reserved nor unapproachable. Let's use *calm* and *peaceful* in lieu of reserved. In every community, some people are sociable, some

reserved; some like to talk, some prefer to lis10; some help and some do not; some are shy and some are bold.

The Gabe Gabriel
Just uh second uhgo ya said dat national generalization is uhlways unfair but ya yarself are generalizin'! Huh---?

The First Woman Voter
Every man is a world, one day happy, the other day sad, one day energetic, another day tired, one day reticent, another day communicative.

King Charles Frederick
Is das Finnland still kolt?

The Swedish Finn
Not that cold any more. In addition, our cars have motor and interior heaters.

King Charles Frederick
If so I should come back to Finnland and install an heir condition system. By the way do you remember mich?

The Finnish Finn
I'm afraid not!

The Emigrant
I remember the first time I visited Baltic Sea in Finland. My first impression was that it's a lake, so calm! In my country, seas roarrrrr and if you stay even 10 meters away from sea line, waves reach you and send you home wet.

King Charles Frederick
How can't you remember your könig?! How about Prince Friedrich Karl?

The Finnish Finn
Not yet.

King Charles Frederick
What about Väino I?

The Swedish Finn
Remember nothing.

King Charles Frederick
It's a shame! Elected as der könig of das Finnland in der Oktober 1918 and renounced the throne in der Dezember 1918, cause I liked to rule over a warmer place. You probably don't remember me, cause I did not set foot in my Königreich. Please visit my throne and krone in Helsinki museum. Please visit. I have a picture of them in my laptop. Let me see where I have saved it….

The Finnish Finn
The Swedish Finn
The First Woman Voter
The First Finnish Immigrant
The Finnish Refugee
The Veteran
The Police Wo-Man
The Gabe Gabriel[9]

The First Woman Voter
Good that we don't have monarchy. I hate continuity.

King Charles Frederick
Don't say that. I could be a good könig for you. I could rule over you for a thousand year. You could be proud to have a könig like me. You could come to my fabulous palast once a week to see me wave hände for you from my palast balconies. Every year on 9 Oktober could be the anniversary of my accession. Memorable celebrations with only millionen of euros of your paid taxes. Fabelhaft! But I wish it was warmer! The celebrations could be more fabelhaft even. And if you liked it, we can have one more celebration on Mai 1 on my birthday. That also might cost only some millionen euros, but since the weather is nice, you willingly would like it, don't you? Do you see how the royal families

gracefully celebrate some days in year in an economical manner? Aha, and if any euros were left, I pay some for charity. The cameramen and reporters accompany me to record such humanitarian moments. Gnädig, isn't it? I establish a department of history of my own with some professional schreiber to write your royal family's history of grace. Then, the next generations will be proud of such a marvelous history. Believe me. It does not cost a lot. 10 schreiber would be enough, and to like their jobs and write satisfactorily we can pay 10 tausende euros per month per person. How much will it cost altogether in a year? I'm not good at math but for having elegance it will be nothing, I suppose.

The Emigrant
I suppose Finns were wise not to have you. Otherwise, they should have added a revolution to their dramatic history.

The Finnish Finn
Right. I'm a man of finnish.

The Swedish Finn
I'm a man of finnish as well.

The Finnish Finn
Sure we are.

The Meta-Medium
The headlice today. In their experiments set up to learn about migration of different species, scientists found that black lories and blue-eyed cockatoos repel each other. In their experiments, they put a blue-eyed cockatoo into the cage of black lories. They observed that black lories took distance from the blue-eyed cockatoo and even to avoid it they changed their paths. Scientists applied this discovery to the redefinition of postrace, endogenous and exogenous relations.

The Emigrant
Bravo! Some scientists really work hard. Right?

The Gabe Gabriel
Wron'

The Emigrant
By the way, do you know that the head of Masculinity Department attacked me once?

The Swedish Finn
Verkligen? Varför?[10]

The Emigrant
Because I greeted her twice in one single day.

The Finnish Finn
The Swedish Finn
The First Woman Voter
The First Finnish Immigrant
The Finnish Refugee
The Veteran

The Emigrant
She lashed out on me, saying "Do you think you look kind if you say HELLO again and again? Wipe that smile off your face-----."

The Finnish Finn
Incredible

The Swedish Finn
Unbelievable

The First Woman Voter
Unimaginable

The First Finnish Immigrant
Unthinkable

The Finnish Refugee
Outrage. It's against sisu!

The Veteran
I'm so sori. It's another story. Wis for your glory.

The Police Wo-Man
Such missfits ruin nice pikcher of finntastic Finnland.

The Gabe Gabriel
KKK. Uh rare one. I've received more dan enaf of both medium and well done.

The Chorus

no skin bet-ween us

colors mished

colors mashed

dark and white

red and yellow

like a rainbow

what colors

become flowers

in $6 \times 31 \times 12$?

mind boggles!

notoriety no variety

variety beauty

beauty equality

The Finnish Finn
Hiljaisuus on kultaa.[11]

The Swedish Finn
Silence!

The Veteran
But do you know that Finland is kuluisa[12], mikä on kuluisa eng-
lanneksi? [13]

--------------------[14]
Well-known

The Chorus
Dear reader and/or audience, would you like to take a short break
and have some refreshments? It's totally up to you. If not, please
take a deep breath. Perfect.

The Veteran
Kiitos, Joo.[15] Finland is well-known for bos its white days and
black nights, sunlight and moonlight.

The Emigrant
To me, a major number of Finns are helpful, hardworking, committed and honest, and one doesn't represent all. One is only one.

The First Woman Voter
But one is enough to ruin our image. By the way, our sun is a bit
shy, isn't she? She doesn't shine all days even in summer. We all
wish to see her but she hides away.

The Meta-Medium
The brea-king news. Scientists have found in their most recent
studies that the small ants have a special appeal for big ones. In
their experiments, they moved a big ant from his nest and located
him in front of a species of small ants' nest. Scientists observed
that small ants were are attracted by the big one and gather gath-
ered around him immediately. They are hopeful to apply this
finding to the redefinition of subgroup and supgroup, subordinate
and superordinate relations.

We have light and darkness in extremes!

The Finnish Refugee
I still love Karjala. My heart is still in Viipuri.

The Veteran
We counterattacked bravely and bogged 'em down.

The Finnish Refugee
Hieno. I do admire yor gallantry.

The Veteran
I lost my life, too.

The Finnish Refugee
I lost my child. Shot dead.

The Veteran
We tried to regain those but were just alone.

The Finnish Refugee
Nice to see you again here.

The Veteran
Hauskaa tutustua.[16] Have you seen this poem:

> l(a
>
> le
>
> af
>
> fa
>
> ll
>
> s)
>
> one
>
> l
>
> iness[17]

The Finnish Refugee
Moved, relocated, removed, rerelocated by force not choice. A vicious cycle, a vicious circle!

The Swedish Finn
We've had a very dramatic history.

The Police Wo-Man
The world history is fool of tragic stories of soljers who did do will not know each other at all but were are killed killing on behalf of zose who knew know each other quiet wel.

The Finnish Finn
Finland was a bit remote from the world center and remo10ess was the reason for our marginality. But now teknologia has changed our geographical location and moved us toward center.

The First Woman Voter
You know what? I hate centeredness.

The Finnish Finn
But I love it. We were [isolated] for so long; isolation is what I hate.

The Emigrant
I also hate [   ] and   marginality.

The Finnish Finn
I don't know why but when I see an alien, I fit him her them into an image I have for him her them in my imagination. It's inevitable.

The Swedish Finn
War and peace, one hundred years of solitude and colonialism, famine and plague, rebellion and invasion, defeats and victories, refuge and Great Migration, independence and progress.

The Finnish Finn
Yes. Hard Times we also had, Heart Times!

The Finnish Refugee
Look at these 24000, 30000, 85000, 300000, 450000. Intriguing!

The Veteran
But after all these hard times, it's time to live and say farewell to arms!

The Meta-Medium
The headlie tonight. The world will become one. The whole borders between countries will be wiped out soon and the world becomes one. There will be only one central government to rule the whole entire world and there will be some federal governors to each part of the world. The candidates can nominate themselves for the post of presidency. This decision is expected to reduce the number of wars and refugees.

The Finnish Finn
O my gosh! I suppose Finns can make great presidents. If our candidate wins, the world will be rauhallinen. No war no more, no piece no more, no piss no more but peace. Then we are no more geographically marginalized. We'll be rite in the world center.

The Swedish Finn
It's in line with *A Mission for Finland* policy.

The Emigrant
Yes for me. Finnish candidate will have my vote but you know what?

The First Woman Voter
What?

The Emigrant
Do you suppose Finnish Society's Equality of Opportunity a de jure or de facto? How about meritocracy?

The Veteran
I love snow in winter. It brings light. It makes by-passers more visible and driving easier. Have you changed your car winter tyres?

Immigrants can be like snow in winter if seen as an opportunity and not a threat.

The Finnish Finn
But they are not integrated. That's the problem.

The First Woman Voter
You know what? I love voting.

The Emigrant
They won't until they are treated as an alien|nation. Note that being an alien and being alienated are different. Having a Finnish citizenship and being a Finn are also different.

The First Finnish Immigrant
I know what he says. I've been an emigrant myself.

The Emigrant
Thanks for your support. What does integration mean? Unity or Uniformity? Does it mean assimilation? If Finnish companies and employers employ immigrants they get integrated but if companies and employers still racist I mean resist and refuse to employ immigrants under different pretexts, yes they are not surely integrated and form nations-within-a-nation.

The First Woman Voter
Sounds right. Let's vote. I love it.

The Emigrant
Willy-nilly immigrants have alived here. They are here. A great force to include or seclude. Up to you. But note that the consequences of your decision can be BIG, BIGGER THAN WHAT YOU RECKON.

The Veteran
The Finnish Finn
The Swedish Finn

The First Woman Voter
The First Finnish Immigrant
The Gabe Gabriel
The Police Wo-Man

The Emigrant
I'm still afraid of heavy lidless gazes of inferiority.

The First Finnish Immigrant
I was afraid of heavy lidless gazes of otherness and alien|nation when I had just arrived in the US.

The Finnish Finn
Suppose Helsinki becomes the capital of the world. But can we make a cool leadership? I wonder what the elephant thinks of our leadership then?

While ripping the page from the typewriter, balling it up and flinging it at the audience

The Gabe Gabriel
I wrote my own narratives. I acted dem too. I voiced and vi-sioned dem. In my plays I argue for black and white equality. I dink exodusters should uhlso write deir narratives. Dis- is uh move from silence tuh voice and vision.

The Veteran
No one can tell your story, tell it yourself. No one can write your own story, write it yourself.

The First Woman Voter
Write right. If you wait for perfection, you would never rite! There is nothing as perfection. Right!

The First Finnish Immigrant
Boyn! Khiya ro srot qsib srot ro khiya. Tab Faulkner koie, "Pa eroi forlt oi qlr oul, yt loi ro mopil tri."[18]

The Finnish Refugee
Sair dfi er yxieben, liet er yxieten. Zareb nyc nyi. Khiyaben oi vionmav. Qsib mebvanet kui maxime: pe conalis chon khin er khiyaber, conalis kalioneb.[19]

The Emigrant
Nie ob khiyaben! Treib eroi uivd, loinec.[20]

The Gabe Gabriel
Please speak English. It's not fair dat ya speak in Migri Lilt tuhgeder. I kin't understand what ya say. By deh way, why Finns duhn't use "please" in deir speech?

The Finnish Finn
Using "please" in Finnish is interpreted as begging rather than being polite and saying "please" will delay the people who are in line just behind you. In Finnish culture wasting someone's time is far ruder than not saying "please." It's more impolite. Efficiency first. So be quick.

The Emigrant
I am righting about otherness. Otherness kills!

The Swedish Finn
Who says otherness bites? Otherness is not always bad. I have vintage of otherness but I love my vantage. Who says otherness means inferiority? I'm a type of privileged other. To me otherness is privilege and I'm proud of my otherness.

The Finnish Finn
The Finnish Refugee
The Finnish Finn
The First Finnish Immigrant
The Finnish Finn
The Veteran
The Gabe Gabriel
The Emigrant

The Emigrant
But I felt feel feeling the shadow of pain from being different and other.

The First Finnish Immigrant
Let's go to sauna. I missed it a lot.

The Chorus

We get hot

Sweat a lot

Cold water is thrown

Right on the hot stone

What a nice lovely sound

Lots of steam all around

Happiness, peace, health

Relix, mix, remix

Enjoying sauna, seating in steam

Losing some weight, this is our dream.

When I just arrived in Finland, I decided to go to a public sauna in our neighborhood. I was the first one who arrived there. I took a shower and entered sauna. After a few minutes, a fully naked man entered. O my gosh! I was shocked. I first thought he was a gay or something, so I prepared to leave, but just in a few seconds, another fully naked man joined us and sat next to him. I thought this is his partner. You know, nudity in my culture is shameful, and to find myself all of a sudden and upon arrival for the first time without preparation in such an atmosphere was shocking. One of them threw water again and again on hot stones which increased tempo dramatically. The heat was horrendous and unbearable for me. It seemed he was gonna kill me and bake himself. The sauna became a hell and I was determined to leave there but he suddenly asked me a question about my nationality. Soon a conversation was formed based on cultural differences and this made me forget about the heat. There I just found that this is a tradition in Finland to enter sauna nakedly. I have talked to people from different nationalities and they confessed that they have been shocked the first time they visited sauna in Finland. A great and memorable conversation happened which made me totally forget about the intolerable heat of the sauna. With that good memory in mind, now I'm ready for the next season.

7. Season Three:

There is a Hole in Everything

We finally found the magistrate. With our icy hands, we filled in several forms. There were a few people there at that time and soon it was our turn to hand in the forms along with some other required documents. One document was missing and that was our marriage certificate. To change our status, they wanted us to hand it in as soon as we could. The certificate was in our home country, so I called my mother-in-law to officially translate the certificate and send it to us. It took about 10 days and we visited the magistrate again. Eventually we received our social security numbers and a paper which later we found was more than a trouble than a help. With registering our residence status "Temporary," we could get nothing, not even a permanent sim card. This condition continued for about two years. Let me say that half a day was enough for us to learn that Finns are really helpful if of course you ask them for help. We also found that a major number of them speak English eloquently, a sign of high literacy in this country. Finntastic!

I visit visited university tomorrow yesterday five years ago today. In our culture, we buy some souvenirs while traveling. Culturally speaking, this is a sign of at10tion. I did buy some for some people whom I expected to meet. First I met with my two supervisors and gave them their souvenirs in the meantime, a handmade wooden vase and a pen box. One of them willingly and kindly accepted it, whereas the other one got it looked at it strangely and asked, "Isn't it a BRIBE?" I was really shocked and before I open my mouth to say yes or no, he put it on her desk and went on "You look thinner than your photo on your MA degree!" I wished she had asked how I've alived to his office and what has have had happened to us before, during and even after our Flight to Finland. His kind colleague who did not expect such reactions from her colleague tried to ease the 10sion by saying, "You know, he has a sense of humor!" and I smiled a wry smile. To me it was a humor of black type. Two persons, two extremes!

The Gabe Gabriel
Why duhya uhlways use "black" for undesirable an' ill-favored thin's? Use uhnoder color for God's sake, for instance *violet* which uhlso implies *violent*-------.

The Emigrant
Right. OK.

The Gabe Gabriel
We have uhlso lived in deh US for uhbout 400 years but ya still call us "African Americans." We are Americans. So please drop African from our prefix in yor research papers and works hereafter. As Invisible Man truly says: "We are Americans, all of us, whether black or white, regardless of what deh man on deh ladder der tells you, Americans" (Ellison 481).

The Emigrant
K. Yritän.

The Gabe Gabriel
Waht?

The Emigrant
I try.

The Gabe Gabriel
Mmmmm. Let's see!

Among people whom I expected to meet was also a PhD candidate from another country. He was not there, so my supervisor agreed to leave his souvenir on his desk with a note of mine. Then my supervisors showed me around and we headed for a restaurant to have lunch or perhaps supper. There we agreed on a date to visit some important parts of university, including university main library and IT office.

I got home right after that, a home that was not a real one yet. But let's call it HOME. I checked my email box and found that that PhD candidate had kindly sent me a thank-you note and offered his warm hands to help us do some shopping! How could I say NO now? We arranged a time and he took us by his car to IKEA, not once but thrice, and even to our surprise he carried all our stuff by his own car and even helped us assemble some of them. To us he was a deu ex machina! In a few days, everything changed. We had a real cozy home. My promise had come true. Life was now more tolerable for us. Later he and I bought two brand new bikes for ourselves and installed them together but unfortunately his bike was stolen in about 10 days right in front of his home!

The Police Wo-Man
Steel, stole, stollen or stooled?

The First Finnish Immigrant
Stolen.

The Police Wo-Man
Stool En?! S tulen? Really?! How? No mater. Go to inshorence kompeni if you have inshorence.

The Emigrant
What else can you do except sending us to insurance companies?

The Police Wo-Man
I also rite reports. Wizout zat you kant get any money and money is honey, you no?

The Emigrant
Yes.

Our department did not have enough space, so I got a desk in another small research hall which seemed to be a sole property of another department! There were six desks in that hall. Two of them were mostly in use, one was empty and two others were not regularly used. I used my desk every day and thus I met those two PhD candidates almost every day. Out of those two PhD candidates, one was nice and the other ice. Two extremes again! The nice one greeted me every day, had always something nice to say and even invited me and my kid to her house to play with her kid which due to my short life there did not happen. The ice
36

one was totally different. If I greeted her, she did not respond. She looked anywhere, up, down, left, right to avoid any eye contact with me and even when I said *hi* she pre10ded to be so *high* that couldn't hear me. Was she shy or just hated me? This question followed by several more questions teased me. What have I done to her? I've just settled in that hall. Was she a xenophobe? What teased me the most was that I had no answer for those questions.

Ice Not Nice

All night white thin snow

Battered our home window

Time of death

Time of deaf

I could not see but feel

Snow on land on hill

Nothing moved but my heart

And the handles of the clock

It had rubble of word

That needed to be heard

But black thick curtains were there

And the words were not bare to ear

I was sleepy too

You know

I was still

I was steel

I could not hear it

Not even a little bit

Tomorrow I removed the curtain

But snow had gone for a burton

Opened the window

Snow no mo

Ice it became

What a nasty game

Ice just ice

Ice not nice

It had no words any mo

No voice no mo

Frozen frigid and dead

I wish I had left my bed

Can I change ice to snow?

Any reverse? Some heat or blow?

Then a voice rumbled up the roof,

Echoic and fluid: "Don't make 'tis goof"

"No, heat kills ice"

"Noo, heed killz lice"

"Nooo, hit killlzz eyes"

But something inside me says,

"Yes heat heed hit can change still steel."

By now, I had faced a complicated situation, a duality. I had some colleagues and classmates. I knew some university staffs and every now and then we bumped into each other in campus, town and shopping centers. I greeted them and some of them refused to reply. They reacted as if we had never met in the whole entire world! So I made a solemn promise to myself not to greet them any more thereafter. But after a few days when we accidentally met again, those persons did approach me and talked for some minutes about anything from weather, death of their cats and birth of their dogs to their goddaughters to mushroom hunting! I did not believe my eyes. Is s|he the same person? What has happened? Am I dreaming? I then changed my mind and decided to greet them warmly thereafter but next time when we met again and I greeted them they acted as if we have never met at all! It was really odd to me, since in my culture either we know somebody or we don't, and if we do then we always greet even very briefly. I really do not know to call it a syndrome or a skill. If a skill, how much drill does it need to be so skillful? If a syndrome, what's its name? After five years, a few of them are still a real mystery to me! One of my Finnish friends who is the warmest and friendliest person I've ever seen in my whole entire life once told me "they are a real mystery to her as well! They are totally unpredictable!" Sometimes they greet you from the other side of street raising and waving both of their hands and sometimes they do not see you just from 10 centimeters away! Psychologically speaking, either a skill or syndrome, it is a type of abnormality. So to greet or not to greet, that was a question for a while. Later I solved this puzzle, taught myself that each person

is a world consisted of different moods. Someone   who
prefers   A   determIned   sIlence   And   dIstAnce   due   to   severAl   reAsons   today
mayapproachandtalkaboutanythingthatmatterstothemtomorrow.

Besides if I set my nicety toward others based on their nice behaviors, this is not goodness but business, a matter of give and
take. I have also learned that sometimes you should be carefree,
carefree of all people who detest you, carefree of all people who
envy you, carefree of all people who play tight and loose with
your feeling; you should have a carefree attitude toward your
plans that were never implemented, a carefree attitude toward all
your efforts that happened to be abortive, a carefree attitude toward sincere friendships that you spent on a wrong person; you
should just smile and pass and let them think that you do not understand but remember you should not always SMILE and PASS.
Sometimes you should STOP and SMILE. Lots of passing is just
like offering them some extra bullets to shoot at you.

I'm really tired now. It's 1:10 am. I also have to change my car
winter tires tomorrow morning so if possible I will continue my
story tomorrow afternoon. Thank you for your patience. Nähdään
pian![21] Please write your comments if any up to now in the lines
below:

I totally forgot what I was talking about. My mind is like a sieve. Alzheimer finally kills me. Just 10 days had passed and I had just set up my computer. Early in the morning, I met head of a department in corridor and greeted him. She looked away. In the afternoon, I heard someone noisily entered our room. The entrance was behind my back. Upon passing my desk, I raised my head and saw that head of department fixing his eyes on me and uncontrollably I greeted her again. Then suddenly he lashed out at me in front of some PhD candidates who were present in the room, saying: "Do you think you get nice by greeting others again and again? Do you think that smile makes you more attractive? Wipe out that smile from your face!

===

===

===

=========================

=========================

========================="

My ears could not hear any more and he was just shouting continuously. For the first time in a fortnight I could see the grin of that icy student. She was grinning from ear to ear. Everywhere was dark to me, darker than our first night here in Finland. I could knock him down with only one punch but then I thought that I'm an academe and not a hooligan, so I chose silence. In fact two improper acts kills man's honor: to shout when you need to be silent and to be silent when you need to shout.

In your opinion, is that a type of vihapuhe[22]?

□ Yes

□ No

Is vihapuhe in your vision a subcategory of racism?

□ Yes

□ No

Have you been a victim of vihapuhe?

□ Yes

□ No

If yes, please write your narrative below:

If no, how would you react if you become a victim of vihapuhe?

My husband had become strangely silent, always drowned in his own thoughts. He did not even at10d university for about 10 days. Strange it was. He was is always full of joy and energy but there was no sign of joy for a while. I asked him several times what is was wrong but he pre10ds pre10ded pre10ding that nothing has had happened and he is was only engaged with his dissertation. That was not the case, I knew know. He is not that clever to hide anything. I'm sure he'll write about it soon. How could I tell my wife? She was just getting used to here and this event could kill her hope. Later and late I read Phil Schwarzmann advising aliens as such when getting a new job or entering a new office:

> For six to eight weeks you should remain as invisible as possible. Finns take a long time to warm up to new people. Any display of extroversion and people will be talking badly behind your back – even a simple "Good morning!" could ruin the office culture. So come in to work a bit early, leave a bit late, nod to people at the coffee machine, speak only when spoken to and be prepared to tell everyone how much you love Finland. (Schwarzmann 128)

The Gabe Gabriel
Ya just said dat generalization is not fair! Dis- is generalization. Uhnyway, what didya duh uhfter?

I left that research hall right after that. Even after five years when I pass by that building, I am haunted by that memory. I had to keep my supervisors posted of what has had happened and I did. No choice. I had to say why I didon't at10d my office. After hearing my narrative, they were quite sympathetic. Later I found that they had asked an eye witness and she had confirmed my

words. Then based on their former knowledge of that guy's behaviors, they talked to him. Later I also learned that she has had a
long record of aggressive and violent behaviors toward other students and even university staffs and accordingly he is totally infamous. My Finnish friend who was sympathetic toward me also
told me how yesterday she had printed out the motivation letter
of an Italian student willing to come to Finland as a visiting re-
searcher, read it out loud in the coffee room and laughed in a
frenzy at his grammatical mistakes! But why my supervisors sent
me to her den upon my arrival? Anyway, my supervisors re-
spected my decision to migrate from that room. I went there late
at night and moved my stuff to a new office.

I shared an office with the nice PhD candidate who helped us do
our shopping upon our arrival. From 8 to 12, I used the office
and he used it in the afternoons. We met sharp at 12 almost every
day to change our shifts and had a short talk. That was enough to
build a stronger friendship between us. He had practically taught
me how helpfulness can bring comfort and hope to other people's
lives and I promised myself to pay it forward.

The opponent is asking another question. Let me answer his
question and get back to you again.

……………… conju'e memories of slave'y including lynching.
Now that we a'e in 21st centu'y, why contemporary African
American write's a'e still drawing upon slave'y issues?

There are too much suppositions in your question for me to give one particular answer but I suppose these writers draw upon the past to philosophize about the present and future. This may reflect Patricia Hill Collins' "irreparable damage" thesis. Collins claims that the damages of the past continue to persist in the present and if not remedied the damages will continue to persist in the future. The current racial inequalities and discriminations afflicted African Americans in today's world show that the past is not past; rather the legacy of slavery still burdens and exhausted stereotypes are still used showing that roots of slavery are still alive and active. Accordingly these writers are warning us that if the roots are not properly and effectively treated, racial discrimination and inequity will continue into the future.

The Gabe Gabriel
Did ya forget uhbout yor promise. We are Americans, for God's sake eliminate "African American" from your vocabulary.

The Emigrant
Terribly sorry. You're right. Thank you for the reminder.

Anyway, during this time, we met meet meeting quite many nice people. Their nice treatments show showed us not to see only the b|sad side. We found nice friends, Finnish and non-Finnish, whom we are proud of now after five years. One of them was a Finnish PhD candidate who always was is there for us, always asking whether we need help, and if yes, she didoes more than enough to the ex10t that we go went speechless, and the other a

Finnish lady who was is warm, caring, knowledgeable, intelligent, friendly and opinionated on a wide variety of subjects that she discusses discussed with a great sense of enthusiasm. I am was amazed at her knowledge on literary subjects which are were not her field of specialty. She is amazing! After my defense session I mean in an hour or so she will give gave me museum cards as cultural gifts which enable us to visit 200 museums in Finland. Such a marvelous person she is. And now that she has found I'm writing this noveramatry, she sincerely shares what she knows about how to find a publisher. We and our friends get together on different occasions, visit each other's homes and have lots of fun together.

The First Finnish Immigrant
Good for you that could make friends so quick. We had troubles finding friends when we alived to the New World. Everyone was new, everywhere was new, we were new.

Right. My kid was still ill. Coughing and some temperature had made it worse. I called and made an appointment with a doctor in public sector. We visited where we expected to visit but when we got there, we found that we were in a wrong place. In fact, there were two clinics in our district and we had to visit the other one! It was 9:50 am and our appointment was at 10! How could we get there? Probably by bus! The nurse who could not speak English at all tried to give me some instructions in Finnish but I got nothing! I just could understand "bussi" in her fast words and long sen10ces. But it was late. How could we get there on time by bus? Shall I call a taxi or something? I was desperately thinking what to do when an old man suddenly approached me and said, "tuolella ilmoitkesli poaraya kundelere terveisekselle turvamesudan kautaminen ya autolla sitten ayaminen ulosala tahdenta liittyymahkohta tai kolminkertaista keino ------------."[23] But I couldn't get him. He could understand from my eyes that I got but nothing. Then he tightly held my hand and dragged me. I thought he wanted to show us the direction of bus stop or the other clinic. It was 9:55. No hope! He led us to car parking, opened the door of a car that was older than himself with his key and pointed us to get into his car. Then he drove slowly. Where are we heading for? Neither he said a word on the way nor could I say anything. In about 10 minutes we found ourselves in front of a huge building. He pointed out to the building. O my goodness! I could see the sign of the clinic. I was speechless! I repeated "kiitos paljon"[24] 10 times and bowed down 10 times. This was what I could do at that moment. Looked at my watch. It was 10:05. We rushed to the clinic, asked info desk about our appointment and they said that the doctor will call you soon. The doctor called us in at 10:10. During the time waiting, I was praying for that old man. I'm still praying for that angel. I wish I knew his name and address and could make up for his attention and affection but I didon't. So I can pay it forward.

It's Friday night and I'm still in lab doing some experiments. My husband and daughter are here helping me. Tomorrow we need to come again to turn off gas cylinder and analyze the results. My daughter is drawing a picture of Angry Birds but I wish she did draw the picture of Happy Birds. A couple of years ago, she received Smiley Statue at school in Finland due to her cheerful and helpful character and I want her to keep it on. The world is lacerated and frustrated of anger and war, isn't it? How would it be if next year *Star War* produces *Star Peace*? As a person who in his childhood has seen eight years of war, lost some of my classmates in bombardments, had no hopes to see dawn at night when I went to bed and dusk in the morn when I woke up with my father losing one of his eyes in that deadly war, I don't like to see any more war on the earth.

The Meta-Medium
The brea-king news is was will be b r e a k i n g. The brea-king news was is will be brok. The brea-king news will be was is broken.

A nice doctor. Our first experience of visiting a doctor in this country. Warm young and friendly. He assured us that she will be recovered soon with his prescription but wanted us to make another appointment if it didn't work. The medication was quite helpful and eased her coughs to a great ex10t but did not totally stop it. We visited him again and he booked an appointment with a specialist who helped my daughter fully recover.

We had to send my daughter to preschool. We visited a preschool in our neighborhood. The staffs were kind and enrolled her in 10

48

minutes. There were only a few months left to the end of school year. My wife was kind of worried about our daughter, since our daughter knew neither Finnish nor English. How can she communicate with her teachers and classmates? But I was quite hopeful, since one of my professors in my home country who had the experience of living and studying in England with his two small kids advised me that his kids picked up English just in a few months and even used to correct his mispronunciations!

She started preschool. Despite my husband's optimism, I was really worried on the first day. When she returned home I was expecting her to cry and say that she never ever at10d that school but against my expectation, she had loved it. My husband was right. She had found some nice friends, however I couldn't understand how they communicated. A couple of days later I visited her school, she was happy and had managed to find some nice friends: Onna, Meri-Tuuli, Ville, Ali. So cute! Her teacher and nurse were also committed and did whatever they could to improve her Finnish and ice-skating! She loved her teacher so much and at home she always talked for hours about her, what she said, what she did, looking forward to seeing her tomorrow.

But this happiness didoes not last long, just for a month or two. One day she came back home sad, saying that her teacher is in hospital and won't at10d school for about 10 days. "She will be back, don't worry," we said. But our remarks changed but nothing. She believed that she won't be back and she was right. To our great surprise, the young healthy energetic smiley nice teacher passed away for unknown reasons. The sad kids held an extremely emotional ceremony at school in their own childish manner that made even a stone cry. Life is transient! No one knows what will happen to us tomorrow.

O my God! I'm defending. I'll have my karonkka tonight and I'll have another lectio in that celebration, so I should keep some breath for tonight as well. I have not even thought about what I'm gonna say tonight. Being so engaged in lots of administrative works left me no time even to review my notes and prepare for my defense let alone thinking about my karonkka speech. But no worries! There would be a couple of hours after my defense and before my karonkka. A month before schools end, we received a letter. The letter asked us to meet with new teacher and school principal during next week. They had a b|sad news for us, saying that since our daughter still has trouble speaking and writing Finnish, she must at10d another school for a while to improve her language skills and then after receiving language certificate, she can be back. How can we tell this to her who loved her classmates and school?

We visited new school right after our meeting, somewhere in city center. I had to take her there every day by bus. Her classroom was located in the fourth floor of an old building, so different from her current school and she had to climb up lots of stairs several times a day. The teacher as expected was kind and friend-

50

ly but I had problems with her new class conditions. It consisted of 10 students from different age ranges, one 7-year-old boy and the others 10 to 12 years of age. The class teacher based on her former experience believed that kids mostly receive the certificate in one academic year! This meant that my daughter will at10d school one year late! Was there any choice?

I got back home and did our best to find a solution for the problem. We asked our colleagues and friends and they introduced International School to us. Good idea! Let's try this. We visited its website, saying that candidates are interviewed. Speaking English was the password which she did not have. The interview for first graders was only three months away! O my God! What can we do in this short period of time! I had have lots of work myself but it is was worth trying it and we dido. We made our kid interested in some useful websites for learning English. My wife and I read some easy story books to her and asked her some comprehension questions. We all dedicated four to five hours a day to this and her progress was incredible.

Soon it was the test day, and since we had no idea about the test level and the questions that might be posed, we were kind of worried. It was her turn to be interviewed. I waited for her out of classroom, walking in corridor, thinking how I could send her to the Finnish school in city center if she fails the interview. She came out after half an hour, claiming cheerfully that she had answered all questions, except one in which the interviewer had asked her about her birth date and she had replied, "I don't know. Please ask my dad." I told her that you had have already answered that question nicely, too! But we had to wait for about 10 days to get the results.

What would you do if you need to wait for about 10 days? Traveling, playing basketball, reading some other books in addition to mine, doing some house chores or what? The hardest thing in the world is to just sit waiting. I've heard that patience is not about waiting but about how well we behave while waiting.

The Finnish Finn
The Swedish Finn
The First Woman Voter
The First Finnish Immigrant
The Veteran
The Police Wo-Man
The Emigrant
The Finnish Refugee
The Meta-Medium
The Gabe Gabriel

And YES she was admitted to International School! We were relieved ☺

Now after five years and as a result of Finnish rich educational system, she speaks English, Finnish and some French and some Swedish in addition to her mother tongue.

6. Panel Two:

A Modest Proposal

The Gabe Gabriel
Mmm. I've uhlso heard uhbout Finnish nice educational system. How loooooooooong we stay in sauna. It's hut up here and I'm not used tuh it.

The Emigrant
I was not used to it but now I am, 'cause inside is dark, and large gust of steam blurs every one's color and class.

The Swedish Finn
Do you mean that sauna changes cc-awareness to cc blindness?

The Emigrant
Yes. You well-worded it. There is no color no class and no gaze. All invisible. A very relaxing place but I don't like something about sauna.

Mikä?[25]

The Emigrant
The arrangement of its seats in three steps! The higher, the hotter; the lower, the wobblier. I love it all in one circular level. Neither rare nor well-done but medium. Ymmärrättekö?[26]

The Gabe Gabriel
Write yor narratives. Write some social plays uhbout yor rights. Dis- is uh move from uhbsence tuh presence. Dis- is deh elixir of immortality.

The Emigrant
Each one, write one you mean? Do you say that we should not be
a real waste of space?

The Police Wo-Man
Aha.

The First Finnish Immigrant
Yes, I was myself an immigrant and have had lots of hardships in
the US, Canada, Australia and Alaska.[27]

The Finnish Refugee
I understand you too. Immigrasion is always hard.

The Emigrant
Oletko poliisi?[28]

The Police Wo-Man
Kyllä.[29]

The Emigrant
My house was burglarized.

The Police Wo-Man
Go to inshorence Kompeni.

The Emigrant
But I know who has done it. Just keep an eye on her for a few
days and you will see.

The Police Wo-Man
Go to inshorence kompeni. Tis is the easiest way.

The Emigrant
But I know who has done it. She is quite infamous in our neighborhood for burglary and prostitution. I also know her two ac-
complices; those who provided her with some info about our
household. Just keep an eye on her and her contacts and you will

54

see. Just ask her what she was doing in our building block on December 8 and two days later when this happened?

The Police Wo-Man
No ifs and butts! I fine you. Here's Fineland.

The Emigrant
But____

The Police Wo-Man
"You case in our polivedepartment and investicator . . . has decided to end investication for now until someting new comes up. You have sent many emails and calls to . . . and now i am telling you that you cant send emails and call alk the time. If something new comes up.. police will call you."[30]

The Swedish Finn
The First Finnish Immigrant
The Finnish Refugee
The Veteran

The Emigrant
But I've never sent any email. I didon't even have their email address. I just called two times. NO one replied and once I left a voice message. That's all.

The First Woman Voter
Really?

The Gabe Gabriel
We have strong police officers here. Dey always stay on top of breaking news. Come to deh US.

The Emigrant
No thanks. Immigrants have come here with high hopes to be effective members of society and build an honorable life for themselves as well but_____

Mine Eyes Have Seen

I eye seagulls leaving

fly in sky

orderly while disorderly

I hear them tell

tell their sweet memories

memories of their hunting

hunting French fries and ice creams in front of fast foods

tell their sweet dreams

dreams of hunting fish

I see seagulls leaving

The Swedish Finn
Vem says otherness means lowness? To me it's privilege and I'm proud of my otherness. Our language is an official one. Don't you see?

The Finnish Finn
I don't under-stand you.

The Emigrant
I don't under stand you, either.

The Veteran
We fought hard. Hard to end up giving 10. 10 is a lot but we did what we could.

The Swedish Finn
Vem says minority means abasement? To me it's privilege and I'm proud of my minority. Look at the street names. Look at my language. Look at me.

The Finnish Finn
The Finnish Finn
The Finnish Finn

The Swedish Finn
Vem says minoritet brings abjection? To me it's privilege and I'm proud of my minoritet. Look at ministers and parliament members from us. I'm educated, cultured and international with social skills.

The Emigrant
Right. We envy you.

The Gabe Gabriel
Have ya read my song "Der is mo' to bein' black dan meets deh eye?" Uh reminder: don't forget tuh write yor narratives. Dis-moves ya from invisibility tuh visibility. We've tried it and it worked.

The First Finnish Immigrant
We have a long history of exodus. Sometimes as refugee from war or famine and sometimes in seek of a better life, I mean a new start.

The Finnish Refugee
I'm one of them. I miss Salla. My heart is still there.

The Emigrant
Life is challenging for new arrivals. Lots of challenges.

The Finnish Refugee
But Finns did a great job, launched a cras' program, resettled us, reconstructed the war-torn country and even managed to pay an amount of repatriasions.

The Emigrant
Your sisu is praiseworthy.

The Finnish Finn
We made kahvi substitute from dandelion roots.

The Swedish Finn
We made shoes out of wood and papper.

The Emigrant
I need only justice, just this and not dis-. Is that a big demand?

The First Finnish Immigrant
I gave them log cabins, but they called me Forest Finn in return! I worked hard as sailor and minor [sic]. I served as carpenter and craftsman.

The Emigrant
The contributions of immigrants are always unseen.

The Gabe Gabriel
Didya notice dat I was last scene uh couple of days uhgaw?

Yes, where were you? You are always on line!

The Gabe Gabriel
My Finnish friend and I went mushroom hunting. When we got tuh forest, 10 mosquitoes uhttacked me. Dey bit all my body! Dey were telling me clearly tuh get out of here. "Here is our realm. Gaw back home, stranger." But my Finnish friend had bug spray so he became immune tuh deir bites. Poor me!

The Emigrant
Good to know that. Spraying is important.

The First Finnish Immigrant
I'm John Morton originally from Rautalampi.

The Veteran
Nice to meet you here. I love your signature.

The First Woman Voter
And I'm Kuku Selma.

The Veteran
Nice to meet you two.

The First Finnish Immigrant
It was hard to get here. I had to book several transit flights. They were expensive; higher than the credit limit on my MasterCard. I had to change my jumbos again and again. 24 hours of flight. I still have jet lag. But still it is much much more convenient than the way I got there. I changed my sailing boats and steamers and ferries several times. I rowed a long way, too. My hands are still numbs. There was a great traffic across the Atlantic Ocean. So many red lights on the way. To get there faster, we even run timbers. I was on water for a couple of months. I was slow to get a bed in a cabin so I stayed in low decks. Lots of people lived and slept there, too small for those number. We even slept on top of each other. It stunk there. I also got sea sick but some of my fellows got infectious dizzizzez and lost their lives on the way. Loooooooooong voyages with mass of immigrants by unequipped vessels made it really unbearable! I escaped by the skin of my teeth.

The Finnish Refugee
I'm originally from Petsamo but still am in love with Vyborg.

The Finnish Finn
I suppose we introduced sauna to them too.

The First Finnish Immigrant
Yes, I built it myself there. We also made some unions. Good reputation we had for our hard work and stamina but bad reputation for our unions in the eye of exploitative employers. We were known as troublemakers for organizing strikes. We were blacklisted. Some employers said that we Finns are good workers but are trouble breeders. When I applied for a job and superin10dent

found that I'm a Finn, he said, "You're good for hard physical labor but you're an anarchist an agitator and I don't want YOU."

The Swedish Finn
Historia repeats itself. It's cyklisk.

The First Finnish Immigrant
Unpleasant images of us grew. Called us wild knife fighter, Jackpine savage, peasants, clannish and commies!

The Finnish Finn
Outrage!

The First Finnish Immigrant
We faced quite a bit of discrimination, race and class discrimination, became the victims of race and class slurs. We were under pressures and had to assimilate. Quick to adopt American life and dress styles. Our women discarded their huivi[31] worn over their hair and began to wear the big wide hats and fancy dresses popular in the US. Our men also put on bowler hats and stiff starched collars above their suit coats.

The Gabe Gabriel
New narrative I hear tuhday. Please duhn't ladle any mo' water on deh stones. I take uh cold shower and might get back. I'm not used tuh heat. Hetkinen.[32]

The Finnish Finn
The Swedish Finn
The First Woman Voter
The First Finnish Immigrant
The Veteran
The Police Wo-Man
The Emigrant
The Finnish Refugee
The Meta-Medium
King Charles Frederick

The Gabe Gabriel
I'm back. Please gaw uhead.

The First Finnish Immigrant
I was telling that we faced race and class discriminations. They said we speak a bizarre language which is non-European. Called us Asian Finn. Have you read Carl Ross's *The Finn Factor*? Called us Mongolian.

The First Woman Voter
Outrage!

The Finnish Refugee
Yes and said under the Asian Exclusion Act we were not eligible to apply for citizensip.

The First Finnish Immigrant
Called us Findian. Called us also China Finn, dumb Finn and Roundhead. Treble experience! I wanted to return home. America was not the kind of gold mine I expected.

The Emigrant
So you've had tearable experiences as such.

King Charles Frederick
Mmmm. Let me say that I'm an immigrant myself but a noble one, selbstverständlich. Immigrants are also of two types: Immigrants and immigrants. Did you know?

The First Finnish Immigrant
I hated such name calling. My kids rejected their Finnishness. They were ashamed of their names, accents and traditions. They wanted to melt in the pot as soon as they could but the pot was extremely cold. Later my daughter married an American guy and you don't know how happy she was to adopt his American surname. I also joined some American clubs and churches and even changed my name to Tom Miles.

The Gabe Gabriel
Tom Miles?! But still dey could find dat you have come from miles uhway, but lucky ya dat could choose yor names. I had tuh uhdopt de sirname of my masters. No choice but force.

The Emigrant
Nice strategy. Will I have more chance to get fund in Fundland if I adopt a Finnish moniker?

The Finnish Finn
The Swedish Finn
The First Woman Voter
The First Finnish Immigrant
The Veteran
The Police Wo-Man
The Finnish Refugee
King Charles Frederick
The Gabe Gabriel

The First Finnish Immigrant
I changed my name. Now I'm Renny Harlin. Does it suit me?

The Finnish Finn
Yes, you are kuluisa nyt. Can I ask for your autograph?

The First Finnish Immigrant
My pleasure.

The Emigrant
After changing my moniker, shall I attach a photo to my CV?

The Gabe Gabriel
We uhlways uhvoid it, 'cause it reduces our chances of even being shortlisted and invited tuh interviews.

The Swedish Finn
Never include it if you don't look Finnish.

The Gabe Gabriel
By deh way, why Finnish gals duhn't keep deir maiden names uhfter marriage? Why men refuse tuh uhdopt deir wives' sirnames? Where are feminists? Why dey show no reactions? It's uh good subject for lots of papers I s'ppose.

The Police Wo-Man
Az far az I red, Fins just like today's emigrants imigrated for many reazonz and fased many chalengez. They weare'll be diskriminated against. The cents of displacement, not being wanted, prejudisez toward them, stereotaipez, name-calling, scense of inferioriti, uncertainti toward fucher, unemployment, unfair treatment killedkill'll kill'em.

The Emigrant
To me emigrants are of two types: those who serve and those who consume. The first group comes to work hard, to prove themselves and to serve society whereto they move, while the second group is like grasshoppers that attack a green plantation and dry it; those who come under different pretexts just to receive some benefits. It's not fair that the taxes of tax payers be spent on such indolent people. But the country needs to favor meritocracy rather than favoritism. Unfortunately as far as I know some of vacant positions publicly advertised have been already filled before they are opened; and it is surprising to see that in many cases persons who have had affiliation with those departments finally are "selected" to fill those vacant positions! It seems that those positions have been opened just for those particular persons, but based on law they have to make the call open to public. It's death, death of hope, death of commitment, death of meritocracy, death of diligence, death of progress, death of life and death in life you know. These types of already filled "vacant" positions just create hopes which prove to be forlorn for other applicants, waste their time and energy and then kill their trusts. Bang Bbang Bbaang Bbaanng Bbaanngg! It's a murder. Last year my Finnish friend who was appointed as a member of a committee to select and employ a professor for their department revealed a secret to me. He said that we received about 10 appli-

cations for 1 professorship post. She then continued that there was one applicant who was much more better than all others in all aspects. She had a great record of publications and teaching experience at different universities in and out of Finland. She had also received her PhD from a top-ranking well-known university out of Finland but our head of department who had opened that position just for her former student used a "clever" strategy along with some different pretexts to dismiss that applicant and he did. How could she employ that applicant while he had opened that position just for the apple of her eyes? Since he himself was a backstabber and went green on former head of department who had highered her, causing long-term internal and external conflicts in that department, she wanted someone safe, totally safe, someone who could be fully obedient, someone who never betrays her. He knew how hard it was for her to become the head of department and did not want to lose it. So priority does not go to quality and development of department but to position safeguarding!

The First Finnish Immigrant
So b|sad. We had the same problem. No matter how good we were there, they also highered obedient workers! They also wanted safe workers. Position, profit, privilege, pleasure and promotion matter mattered. History repeats itself!

The Emigrant
In fact, positions are opened because some apples of the eyes are positionless and some poor naïve appelsiinis take those public calls seriously, spend some time and energy to fill in the forms, to write research plans and motivation letters. They also need to ask for recommendation letters which also kills the time of referees but at the end of the day the apples come out, no matter how good and tasty and nutritive those appelsinnis are were. Have you heard "an apple a day keeps the doctor away?" That means an apple will prevent other talented persons to become useful doctors. Mine Eyes Have Seen! Mine Ears Have Heard! Bang Bbang Bbaang Bbaannng Bbaanngg! It's a murder, murder of meritocracy, murder of progress, murder of hope, murder of tal-

ent. It's also a birth, birth of favoritism, birth of connection, birth of disparity, birth of nepotism. Some of these apples after FIVE years of receiving grants and salary have failed even to produce one chapter of their dissertations let alone being able to have any publications! But who cares? Who observes? Today I mean yesterday another apple graduated after THIRTEEN years! Once I told her that if he persists and continues steadfastly for just a few more years, she will retire as a PhD student; I mean he will really live up to the real meaning of JATKO------------------------------opiskelija. But no worries! Right after his graduation, a teaching position was opened especially just for her, lest he remains positionless! Several other appelsiinis as usual applied for that position but as it was serene like blue sky and bright sea he was had been "selected" for that position. Bang Bbang Bbaang Bbaanng Bbaanngg! Three other soft murders, because with those grants and salaries that she received during thirteen years of PhD studies, two more doctors could graduate, and one further soft murder for the new position that he received while he did not deserve. Who cares? Who observes? Once I visited a Finnish organization and read these lines to its responsible staff; he sighed, nodded and said, "Unfortunately that's true! Many Finns and non-Finns have told me this while visiting my office." So what? You should observe what is happening and stop the wrong trend. To "fight" this, some foundations in Finland have devised a ………….. way. They have added a new page to their online application form and have released names of their board of trustees asking applicants to declare whether they are related in some way (also through marriage) to any of those people or to their spouses? This question as one of my friends says is like the question in the forms we are asked to fill in upon entering the US: "Are you a terrorist? If not, are you related in some way (also through marriage) to a terrorist?" What the heck? Who says YES? And is the circle of proximity only confined to applicants' relationship with the members of board of trustees and their spouses based on marriage? How about their neighbors and their dependents? Their colleagues and their dependents? Their friends and their dependents? . . . . This proximity question by itself is problematic raising doubts toward board of "trustees." Almost all open positions or foundations that welcome applications state or have to state something like: "We are committed to promoting equality and preventing discrimination in all its operations." Nice words but actions always speak louder than words!

The Veteran
Very dreadful.

The First Finnish Immigrant
How s|bad! I know what you say. Anyway despite my children, my grand grandchildren are proud of their Finnishness. They are proud of what their parents were ashamed of or neutral about. They search for their roots and dig for dignity in their past, history, culture, tradition and customs.

The Swedish Finn
There are shocking news of the refugees right now in the news. Let's turn on The Meta-Medium.

The Chorus
Man without food lasts one month

    without water one week

        without air one minute

            without Tea Vea one tick

                without internet less than a tick

The Finnish Finn
Who says that? During summertime, I abide within my summer cottage for a month or two without even electricity, let alone internet-yhteys.

The Gabe Gabriel
So if ya submit uh paper tuh uh journal and deh journal sends ya back reviews wid uh one-month deadline tuh uhpply deh comments and resubmit, what duhya duh?

The Finnish Finn
Kesä möki on tärkeämpi.[33] That brings tranquility, relaxation, nostalgia, family reunion if and if it is not an inheritance shared by your siblings and their exxxxxxxxxx10ded families!

The Veteran
Living in a summer cottage without electricity, internet and running water while you need to fight against mosquitoes, cut grass, chop wood, clean cottage and so on for a couple of mons [sic] make you totally frustrated and make you miss city life.

The First Finnish Immigrant
I showed them deforestation techniques and construction skill of log cabins but they called me Forest Finn in return!

The Meta-Medium
The headlive today. Over one million refugees have made their way to here escaping conflicts in their countries. Many people arrived yesterday arrive today or will probably alive tomorrow after perilous sea voyages. Many of these displaced people are children who need special protection. At the same time the wreck of a fishing boat that sank a couple of days ago were found, drowning hundreds of refugees packed on board. The disaster is feared to have killed up to 1000 people making it one of the deadliest shipwrecks in decades of seaborne emigration from there to here. Navy has recovered 100 bodies but hundreds of corpses are believed to be trapped below deck where survivors said emigrants, including many women and children, were locked. Also according to some news agencies anti-emigrant vigilante hate is dramatically rising and hatred toward emigrants has increased by 40% during the last two years.

The Gabe Gabriel
Deh Middle Passage is still der in(t)act.

The First Finnish Immigrant
I've passed some of these pass ages. Let's say Middle Passages.

The Finnish Finn & The Swedish Finn
Whose fault? Not mine. Whose blame? Not mine.

The Emigrant
Imagine there is an ant nest near your house and they are doing nothing to you. What happens if you throw some oil into their nest?

The Finnish Refugee
They leave their home and move toward yours. I was doing my own life. Someone poured oil to mine.

The Emigrant
People were doing their own life. They said will say saying he must go, cause they dido not like him and he didoes not go then they threw throw throwing oil into their nests.

King Charles Frederick
What do you mean by throwing oil? Oil matters. How kaan we throw it away?

The Emigrant
Sorry, it was not a good example. They threw throw throwing BOMB.

The First Finnish Immigrant
Do you know that I served as Alaska's governor for two five-year terms altogether 10 years? I then changed my name to Amy Kaukkonen and served as mayor of Ohio.

The Emigrant
Really? Name changing works a lot. I'll change mine. Does Senja Siltala suit me?

The Veteran
It would be better that your surname ends in –nen. Why don't you adopt "Makkarainen." We Finns love makkara and your new surname enlivens nice memories of grilling makkara for boards

of trustees while they are reviewing your application. This might increase your chances. Senja also signifies someone who is kind and hospitable to aliens. Right-wing party is hot now, so you'd better adopt another name. How about "Aava?" Aava Makkarainen? Sounds good.

The Finnish Finn
Instead of Makkarainen, choose Suomalainen.

The Swedish Finn
Pick a Swedish name. How about Nylund. It's really prestigious.

The First Woman Voter
Shhh. Let's see what the Meta-Medium says.

The Meta-Medium
The headlice today. Two million refugees have made their way to here, escaping bloody conflicts in their countries. Many people alived yesterday and many more are expected to alive today and many many more will be expected to probably alive tomorrow after perilous sea voyages and land journeys. Many of these displaced people are women who require special protection needs. At the same time the wreck of a fishing boat that sank a couple of days ago were found, drowning hundreds of refugees. The disaster is feared to have killed up to 1010 people making it one of the deadliest shipwrecks in decades of seaborne emigration from there to here. Navy has recovered 110 bodies, but hundreds of corpses are believed to be trapped below deck. Also according to some news agencies anti-emigrant hate is significantly increasing and hatred toward immigrants has risen by 50% only during the last year.

5. Season Two:

Wake the Dead

It was getting warm. The nature was so beautiful. Yellow dandelions on green leaves of grass, a nice combination, isn't it? But it lasts for only 10 days, since they mow the lawn and all poor dandelions are beheaded! Soon everywhere becomes only green, monocolor! I love the combination of dandelion and grass, yellow and green, as well as other colors all mixed to make a garden. I had brought three suits and three ties from my home country, two of them are still untouched. One day I decided to put on one of them, a black one. On the way to university, people fixed their in10se gazes at me with their eyes undimmed as if I had come from Mars. For a while I tried to gaze at their gazes but the level of their gazes was so high that after a few minutes I started asking myself what's wrong with me? Am I handsome or what? If the former, why a few also smirk? I supposed that some of them even saved with their minds what they lost with their eyes to have a subject to share with their companions. Some had sunglasses and hid their gazes but I could still detect their gazes. As soon as I entered a less crowded lane, I took off my dark blue tie and walked on. It made a little change but gazes were still in place, so in the next round I took out my coat and it helped a lot in decreasing the level of gazes. Later I learned that dry cleaning is crazily expensive here so a T-shirt or a shirt plus a pair of jeans possibly from some materials that need not ironing would be the solution to skip laundry high costs. A black suit and a tie is enough for your whole entire life and can be worn on all formal occasions. I love it. This is comfort.

Here Stockmann, which is a well-known expensive brand, is always crowded; however, it happened a couple of times that I told some of my Finnish friends how their shirts or boots suit them and they immediately retorted that they have bought them from Man-hat-10.

The Emigrant
Man-hat-10? Wov! When did you go to Man-hat-10?

The Finnish Finn
A couple of days ago. We usually go there for shopping. I love that.

The Emigrant
Is it nice?

The Finnish Finn
Yes. I love it. I buy many of my and my kids' clothes from there.

The Emigrant
Good for you. How often do you visit there for shopping?

The Finnish Finn
Thrice a year.

The Emigrant
Marvelous! I've heard about Man-hat-10 nights.

The Finnish Finn
It is closed at night. It works from 9 to 6. We can go there next time together.

The Emigrant
Together?! I'd love to. Which airline do you usually use to fly there and how much does it typically costs?

The Finnish Finn
Fly?! We can walk together.

The Emigrant
Walk?! No thanks. I cannot walk from here to home, so how can I walk from here to Man-hat-10?

The Finnish Finn
It's only a 10 minute walk.

The Emigrant
What?! Are you kidding?

The Finnish Finn
No, I'm dead serious. It's down this street.

The Emigrant
What are you talking about?

The Finnish Finn
Man-hat-10 shopping center which sells second-hand stuff.

The Emigrant
The Emigrant
The Emigrant
The Emigrant
The Emigrant

As far as I have seen, a great number of Finns avoid showing off or keep up with the Joneses. They are not also consumerists and still use their 1990 beige Ford Orion even if they afford buying a brand new one. I admire this as well.

Since having an office for four hours a day was not sufficient, I moved to a new office located in university main library. It was a long narrow corridor with 10 very small private offices or rather cells. Some were are still empty. You could see no one there, silent and peaceful. It helped me concentrate and work even during weekends. I wrote many of my chapters and papers while I was there but I was lonely. No one to talk to no one to meet with. I called it corridor no. 10 and wrote the following poem while I was there:

10

mAn	withOut	mAn
bArrener	thAn	wAstelAnd
vOider	thAn	vAcancy
lOner	thAn	sOlitude
even	withOut	shAdOw
hArder	thAn	stOne

[cAptured in mendIng wAlls]

whO's	tO	blAme?
whAt's	the	rejOinder?

fight on, before long, comes the song.

By that time, my wife had got a PhD position. She was lucky and I envied her. She had has two supportive open-minded supervisors. The main one is now rector of a well-known university in Finland, a gentleman with a smile who is proud of having students and researchers from many different countries in his department and now in his university, one who believes in the advantages of multiculturalism, one who values the contributions of his international staff, one who is totally different from those who called souvenirs bribe and wanted to wipe out smile from faces! Again two extremes! Accordingly, he had has had a dynamic department university with lots of marvelous people, programs, meetings and get-togethers on different occasions. I love that dynamism, worldview and openness I always pray for him. The presence of such angels makes the world prettier.

But I did not like the gloomy atmosphere reigning over that corridor. There were about four or five researchers who regularly at10ded there but no one talked to no one. I thought a lot about how I could change that atmosphere. "Sport would make it!" I thought. I visited sport office of university on that day and booked a basketball court for one season. To have it for one year was is really cheaper but I was not certain whether the plan will have a successful outcome. I paid the fee and then put up a notice on the main entrance. By this time one of my caring friends from our department got one of those small offices in that corridor and moved there. Against my expectation, I received a very warm feedback. Two colleagues joined us and the others kindly approached me and thanked me for the idea. Their other plans either overlapped with the basketball event or basketball was not their favorite sport. But that was the beginning of our friendship.

The narrow corridor was no longer narrow. It became wide. The new friends who turned to be my old ones were supportive and caring. They help helped me a lot and we had have had lunch or coffee together. They even held a surprise birthday party for me. Wow, what can be better than that? We needed some more players, so some of my friends also joined us. My wife also asked some of her friends and colleagues and they kindly made the event warmer and more joyful with their at10dance. The event is still continuing after 5 years. Many people have come and left but the event is still in-t-act.

*

Smile please

Cool

Try to keep it on

For the whole day

No one is that poor not to have a smile to offer

&

No one is that rich not to need a smile to receive

*

It was for about a few days that I had some ache in one of my teeth. It was not a serious one but every now and then I had some ache. I called public sector. The system is was in both Finnish and Swedish, so I decided to choose Finnish and there I found I'm number 23 in line! With every countdown I felt like a victor. When I reached number 5, the call was suddenly cut off!

The Swedish Finn
Press no. 2. That's only for the Swedish Finns. You will be no. 2 in line, but first you need to adopt a Swedish name.

The Emigrant
Really?! I didn't know.

What's wrong? I dialed again. I wish I was as fat as my per-sis10ce. I failed. Later I found that my credit on my sim card was over. "I'll top up my credit over the phone and call again tomor-row," I decided and I did. This time I was number 5 in line! I was happy that I've lost nothing. The waiting time would be the same, because just yesterday there were 5 people before me as well! Anyway, it was my time and I started with "Good Day!" Operator tried to inform me that she can't speak English and will ask one of her colleagues to call me back. But thanks to her poor English. What if she had said that in Finnish and hung up on me!

It was around 12 that someone called me with a nice American accent. At first I thought she is calling from US embassy but then she informed me that she is calling from dentistry public sector. I now know why it took them this long to call me back. They had tried to find someone with the best possible accent in their sys-tem. Then she asked about my problem and I explained the ins and outs of my problem, when it started, how it started, how much pain I have, how of10 it comes to me, etc. So far, so good! Then she wanted me to wait for a minute. While waiting, I was looking at my calendar. "I have a couple of courses tomorrow and I can't take tomorrow at all. The day after tomorrow but is perfect. I have neither a course nor a deadline," I was thinking. My calendar review was interrupted by her voice asking, "Does December 10 at 10 am work for you?" "What? But now we are in mid-September!" "Ya, but that's the first available slot we have." What could I do? "OK, let's have it." I wish I was as fat as my patience, too! I marked this important date in my calendar.

Too much sitting is a dangerous thing. Since my karonkka, I've decided not to drink tea or coffee, so let me have a glass of milk. As a result of that decision, I feel healthier. How about you? Would you like to have a cup of coffee? Are you a type of person who thinks a good day starts with coffee, continues with coffee and ends with coffee? I'll get back soon to write the rest of it. Sorry to interrupt!

Why so late? Three months!? Are dentists on strike or something? Soon after three months the important date and time arrived. Three months flew by just like that. By this time my ache had been worsened. I visited dentist and he gave me a frozen icy shoulder. The dentist could not speak English not even a simple sen10ce! He looked into my mouth and immediately said, "The iz rong no" moving his hands to emphasize his message. To say

78

this he also asked his assistant who could not speak English, either. I was just thinking how he has got a degree in dentistry without being able to say a simple sen10ce like that. Has he read any essays on dentistry in English? Does he look into new articles published in the field of dentistry to familiarize himself with new discoveries or does he still use old ways of observation to find out problems!? That was no time for such thinking. I had to respond. "But I have pain. So if there is nothing wrong, why I have pain and is even getting worse day by day?" He did not seem to understand what I said but angrily put a x-ray protection pad round my neck, a slide in my mouth and captured an image amid my coughs.

After a few minutes, he returned and repeated that "the iz rong no." But I had ache. Right after that, I at10ded an international conference in Poland. It was a painful and distressing three-day conference. As soon as I got back, I called the public sector again. This time thankfully operator could speak English and after learning about my killing ache she kindly made an emergency appointment just for tomorrow morn. I arrived in clinic in time waiting for dentist to call me in but when he opened the door all my hopes vanished all of a sudden. To my great surprise I saw that he was he and she was she again! What the heck! How hapless I was am. How was is it possible?! He looked into my mouth without asking me about my dental problem. In fact, it was pointless to ask me because we couldn't understand each other. Then he furiously repeated that "the iz rong no" but the ache was killing me. After he saw discon10t and protest in my face, he unwillingly started to drill a tooth and as soon as his drilling job was over he wrote a phone number on a piece of paper gave it to me and said, "go kal." He also used some gestures to show what he means. I found that I should call and make another appointment for the treatment continuation. I had still ache. Nothing had changed. I got home and called that number to make another appointment. That was the number of the public sector, the number that people should call to book an appointment with dentists. "I get a time probably for tomorrow," I thought. I was number 10 in line. Operator again searched in the system and said that the first available slot is in two months. "What?!" I insisted and explained how important it is to get my painful drilled tooth treated as soon as possible but to my surprise she said that the dentist has recorded in your online profile that there is nothing as emergency! What?! Pain is killing me and the painkillers!

The Finnish Finn
Incredible

The Swedish Finn
Unbelievable

The First Woman Voter
Unimaginable

The First Finnish Immigrant
Unthinkable

The Finnish Refugee
Outrage

Sure, it was. The ache continued and during midnight it was really killing me. Having two painkillers together at a time even did not help. My wife was in a conference in Austria. My daughter was asleep. The pain was killing me. I left home and did drive to some dental clinics I knew and they were all closed. I was the only car in the streets. Suddenly I saw a police car. I stopped them and asked them whether they know knew any open dental clinic for emergency issues and they had no idea. Right now that I'm writing this, I see a police car passing by our house! A nice coincidence. I left my car in a lane and started walking to soothe my pain, still worried what happens if my kid wakes up and finds me not. This concern made me return home immediately. Pain and sleeplessness were my guests till morn!

Early in the morning, I visited a private healthcare sector. To hear that their dentist can visit me right now was the best news I could hear at that time. The dentist called me in, lis10ed to my story at10tively while a light music was on, captured an x-ray and said that the former dentist had drilled and damaged a sound tooth, I mean a wrong one, and not the one that had caused the great ache! She did a great job and that night I had a good night sleep. I went there several times to treat both the damaged tooth and the painful one and each time the bill was extraordinary in a very real sense. She recommended me to file an appeal against that uncommitted dentist and said that she can offer some evidence and bear witness against his work damaging my tooth. My Finnish friend and colleague in the corridor also told me that she will do whatever she can to support me against such an irresponsible figure. She introduced a website to me and encouraged me to make an appeal as these types of good-for-nothings should be eradicated from the face of this country. "Alien & Appeal?!" I already knew know the drill. Once I dared to make an appeal on another issue and the way they handled it was funnier than you can imagine. I made an appeal and with several reasons I stated that A is not fair and should change to B. Upon receiving my appeal they said that it takes about a month to get an answer and I agreed but after a week they keep me posted that A is ready and can be collected! When I went there, I said that A is what I have objected and I wondered why they have spent all this time to finalize A for me while the decision of my appeal might change this. With a smile they recommended me to take A and *if* the result of appeal was positive they will change it to B! A clear sign saying do not waste your time and energy. No choice (=#=) No voice. I got it and then after a fortnight they sent a mail to my home stating that the result of your appeal was negative – stating no reason – and this decision cannot be appealed. That's that! Right from the time that they delivered A to me it was clear like day that I was entangled in a funny game. This reminded me of the way The Venus's case in Suzan-Lori Parks's play *Venus* was treated in court. The climax of this tragedy I mean drilling and damaging my sound tooth happened next week when I received a bill from the public sector!

Anyway, my days were are spent on my research; minority and ethnic literature with a focus of African American literature, quest/ion of identities, feminism, raceless and postrace drama. This affected my life and mind a lot. I was distressed with African Americas' narratives of misery and delighted with their unity and solidarity to fight for their neglected rights. Long hours of my life were are spent in my office and in libraries, doing research, reading, writing and submitting papers to journals. It was winter again, 'scold so I went to my office in darkness and left it in darkness! In the meantime, I at10ded some courses. I tried to be an active member of courses and thus I read the materials quite well in advance to be able to participate in class discussions, comment and ask my questions. As a result, those courses were rich, participatory and fun for me. However, I was so immersed in my field of research that I had no time to take any Finnish courses.

By this time, we had missed home a lot. Home sweet home! Oma koti kullan kallis suomeksi. We decided to buy tickets to visit our home during New Year holidays but since this decision came too late, the tickets were really expensive. Eventually, we found some tickets with more reasonable prices from Arlanda airport, Sweden. We did buy some tickets from Viking Line as well to get to Stockholm. So happy that we are were visiting our home, parents, families and friends! They were are also delighted to see us soon. The countdown for this great reunion had started. We were getting get on board early in the morning and our flight from Arlanda airport happened happen at night. We had about five hours to get to the airport from the harbor. More than enough!

The First Finnish Immigrant
Good that you can visit your home country whenever you miss it. It was really demanding for us to visit Finland when we missed it —.—

The Emigrant
That's very true.

The date and time arrived in the blink of an eye. Happily, we got on board and found our cabin. We had a long voyage ahead. Since we had got up quite early, we had a short rest. At about 10 am, we did some shopping from ferry's duty free shop and decided to have lunch in the ferry's restaurant but it was too early. We decided to look at the partly-frozen sea from ferry deck and take some photos. It was really cold and we could not stay on deck for long. Just upon leaving the deck, we heard a hitting or striking sound, Talah! Tallagh! Tallaagh! O my gosh! What happened? But the ferry was heading for its destination. Perhaps it was an "ice." Ice not Nice. No worries! These ferries are commuting between these countries for about 60 years and nothing thankfully has seriously ever happened.

The ferry suddenly stopped. There was something wrong. It will get solved hopefully, I thought. In a few minutes, peace was pieced and pissed and gave way to turbulence. The duty free shop was immediately closed and the ferry staffs did not allow passengers to enter their cabins. They also started evacuating the cabins. Soon all ferry passengers crowded on decks and in restaurants. The loudspeakers were saying something in Finnish and some passengers rushed to take some life jackets. Some youngsters sang *Titanic* song loudly together, hugged each other bidding farewell. Their *violet* humor created some stress for elders. I could clearly see panic in their eyes.

The Gabe Gabriel
Good job to replace black humor with violet one.

The Emigrant
You're welcome.

We just looked at people running here and there. What has happened? Let me ask the info desk. When I got there, there were about hundreds of people in three lines waiting to ask their questions. The ferry did not move at all. In a few minutes, some helicopters appeared flying over the ferry. Later I learned from some passengers that the ferry's navigator ran out of order and accordingly the ferry stroke some rocks and ran aground!

Why in *No Place to Be Somebody* Gabe Gabriel reso'ts to writing and acting his own wo'ks?

Through writing and acting, Gabe finds the possibility to express his own discourses. This is a way toward self-definition which creates the ground for his definitions to emanate from within rather than without. Writing and acting also help him make his narratives good for the eyes as well. In other words, through writing and acting, he gains independence. Writing and acting also provides the ground for him to reconstruct images of blackness in order to subvert the dominant negative images operating within society. In a broad sense, as a people given to orality because of their circumstances in the US, African Americans are thus the heirs of stories and histories that are for the ears and not for the eyes. Writing is of high importance for African Americans because it converts speakerly to writerly and makes stories and histories good for the eyes. Writing makes them the heroes of their own tales and sustains their survival, struggle and vigilant resistance. In addition, writing as a form of cultural and historical production can challenge the ways through which knowledge and power are constructed, can exchange ideas and allow many narratives to arise.

We looked at our watches again and again. We still have three hours if the ferry starts out right now. Good time to get to airport, no worries, I thought. We have two hours and half. No worries. We still have two hours. We will arrive on time. We have one hour and half. No worries. We catch a taxi from harbor to airport. There were around thousands of people on the decks and in the restaurants. Soon we learned that the problem is worse than what we expected but we were still hopeful. Continued looking at our watches, telling ourselves that we will make it and alive on time. The ferry staff informed people that they can eat in the restaurants for free. I looked at the faces of some passengers, those who had come on a 24-hour weekend cruise were extremely happy, free reception, longer voyage and more fun. However, some faces like ours hosted sorrow. Several small boats approached us. I observed them. There were several divers in orange who dived into the frozen sea to inspect the conditions of the ferry. I was still hopeful.

The Veteran
Why are you that much hopeful? You'll miss your flight I know.

The Emigrant
Really? Oh no!

From 10 am to 10 pm the ferry did not move not even a millimeter. We had made the brea-king news. Some of my friends who knew about our journey called us from Finland which increased our stresses. No choice, let me call the flight agency but how could I? The deck was extremely noisy and I could not even clearly hear my wife talking half a meter away. But no choice. I had to call and I did. Operator asked more than 10 questions for identification: our flight number, our destination, names of passengers, dates of our birth, my credit card number and its security code. I could not hear him and after each question, I had to say

"Pardon?" He repeated and I repeated, "Pardon?" Then I asked to rebook our flight for tomorrow night but he said that all flights unfortunately are fully booked and the next free flight will be in 10 days. "10 days?!" What shall we do?

Desperately, I cancelled our flight, nothing else I could do at those critical moments. Our condition was awful. Many passengers were exhausted by now. We had no access to our cabin for more than 12 hours, lots of noise, lots of stress and distress. How can we inform our parents who are were coming to airport tomorrow? Soon the loudspeakers said something in Finnish and people stood up and cheered up. Perhaps the problem is solved and we move toward Stockholm but there was no point in arriving in Stockholm at midnight. I just saw a man in navy uniform. I desperately approached him but he said that he is super busy at the moment and will get back to me in about 10 minutes or so. We sat there waiting for him.

It's time for our visa extension again. We have to apply for visa annually. We have to fill in several forms, take new photos, receive bank statements, collect some documents, book an appointment though police online system, visit police station, being interviewed and finger printed, pay its fees and wait for three months to receive our new visas.

He showed up some time later. When he found that we are were extremely distressed, he invited us to his own office. He lis10ed carefully to what we said and then apologized for any inconvenience caused. His sense of understanding and sympathy was appreciative. He clearly explained that the ferry will be towed to Maarianhamina. We arrive there in a couple of hours and passengers will sleep in their cabins till morning. Then in the morn some passengers will be sent to Stockholm if they wish so and others will return to their departure city. As for our flight, he promised to contact someone in Viking Line headquarter in Maarianhamina to take care of our tickets but wanted us to meet him again tomorrow at about 10 am to follow up our case. Another sleepless night went by. Later I found that this nice angel was is the ferry's restaurant manager.

I met him at about 10:10 am. He apologized for his tardiness, saying that he was is too busy. He was right and I fully understood his condition. His gentle manner gave us hope and peace of mind. I told him that "Finland should be proud of committed people like you" but from his facial expression I found that he did not like my expression! What was wrong with my expression? Isn't he Finnish or what? He dialed a number and wanted me to talk to his colleague who was in charge of Viking Line insurance related matters.

The Police Wo-Man
I love inshorence. It works at all times, you sea?

The Veteran
Right.

For a few minutes, she was just apologizing and thanking us for our patience. Her kind words showed that we had observed sisu thus far. She assured us that we arrive home by afternoon and then we can contact her for tickets rearrangement. But how about our families in our home country? We should call them right now; otherwise, they go to airport. We did. No choice. All their joys suddenly went away but our promise to do our best to find some tickets as soon as possible made them hopeful.

We were having tough time. The memories of those moments and events even now that I'm recounting them bite me. But accidents always happen! We got home sad and dead tired! My kid fell sleep like a log but how could we? I called that lady and she suggested us to find some proper tickets and make the required rearrangements and then send her our bills so she will refund us. So we started searching in two laptops simultaneously. The New Year was close and the prices were booming minute by minute. There were no tickets from Stockholm to my home country but there were some from Helsinki for tomorrow. The prices were at least three times more than the tickets we had bought some months ago. Will they reimburse for them if we rebook such expensive tickets? I called her again. She had no idea and had to ask their insurance company so she wanted us to call her again.

The Police Wo-Man
Inshorence kompenies are suportive in Finnland; otherwize I koud find real problems in my job.

Yes, they accepted! We tried several times to pay the fee with our credit card but there was something wrong! Payment failed. After several trials and errors, we found the reason. The price of tickets was higher than my credit card ceiling! What could we do? To visit my bank and ask them to increase our credit so that I would be able to buy the tickets but it was late and everywhere was closed! So much stress. The tickets are sold out or prices would go higher by tomorrow even if my bank would agree to increase my credit card ceiling. Will Viking Line agree with the new prices? I called that lady again to notify her of the problem and ask her this question but she did not reply. Another harsh sleepless night passed.

Right now, I am in my supervisor's office to finalize my dissertation. We also need to discuss who should serve as pre-examiners. I had no idea and told my supervisors that I'm ok with whoever they wish. Soon or late I have to visit our Faculty's office to hand in my dissertation manuscript. Our administrative officer received it kindly but she still needs my confirmation for the choice of pre-examiners. I'm sending I mean I sent an email to her. Then I learn learned learnt that I have to wait for three months. No problem for me as I have a lot to do but isn't it too much for you to wait for three months? But anyway thank you for your patience in advance.

I am submitting some papers during the three-month waiting time. I submitted my 10th one today. This number 10 seems to be in my fate. It's always with me wherever I go and whatever I do! I should get rid of it. To this end, I have to work harder, I have two more months to go and planned to finish writing and submitting a paper a month. I feel lots of ache in my back. Too much sitting is a dangerous thing. In the meantime, I received some revisions on a paper I had submitted earlier and I have only one month to apply those comments and resubmit it. What a boring cycle: "write, submit, reject" or "write, submit, resubmit, reject" or "write, submit, resubmit, reresubmit, reject" or "write, submit, resubmit, accept" or "write, submit, resubmit, reresubmit, accept." I also have had a suffocating experience of this type: "write, submit, resubmit, reresubmit, rereresubmit, accept." These are the best possible conventional cases. And after acceptance, you should be really patient, since it takes months or even years for your paper to appear in journals. I have had other type of chocking experience as like I have submitted a paper to a journal and waited for seven months with no reply. I have sent them an inquiry and they did not reply. I sent another inquiry and they got back to me saying that the paper has been rejected; for what reason? Not clear but why not keeping me posted of its rejection? "We receive tons of papers every day, and we have limited number of staff and thus we have limited amount of time to send email to all authors whose papers are rejected!" "What?!" Seven months of my life missed for someone's irresponsibility and lack of commitment and I have to start from the first square.

Three months passed and I submitted my twelfth paper. Please keep your fingers crossed for me.

Early morning we set off for my bank and asked for my credit limit increase. It was not as easy as we imagined. I had to fill in some forms and wait for a while for the bank authorities to review my conditions and make their decision. Waiting kills! Who is to blame? Several 10 minutes of stressful moments passed. What is will be their decision? What shall I do if they say "impossible!" I was anxious. After half an hour, they called me in again. I looked at their faces while walking toward their office. Stern faces they had. The answer is no, I know. No worries, perhaps there is blessing in disguise and we'd better forget about this trip. I remembered my friend who once advised me that if you start an activity and face lots of challenges, stop it! Your destiny is sending you a clear message that this is not a right choice for you. Tread another path. I could feel the symptoms of fragility in myself. An irritating continuous cough had started. We'd better cancel or postpone this wayfare.

Against my expectation, the answer was yes, a killing yes! We just rushed to my office, opened the airline website, entered the dates in a frenzy of anxiety and waited! It was too slow. Yes, there were some tickets still available for today afternoon at 5:30 pm. Ticket prices had boomed compared to yesterday. I looked at computer clock. It showed 12. I wish it was 10 am. I wish we were at home. I wish the ferry had arrived safely on time. I wished I was not coughing. I wished I was not —.— How can we get home, collect the luggage, head for coach terminal and be at Vantaa airport at about 4:30 pm, forget about lunch?! But no choice, all tickets until three days had been sold out! Let's make another risk.

Based on you' studies, can we label Go'done's *No Place to Be Somebody* a drama of trauma?

Yes, probably a soft or mild type of drama of trauma rather than a hard or harsh one, since Gordone's play exposes dark dystopian societies wherein power articulates the socio-economic class, human relationships and even social justice; dark dystopian societies in which systems of oppression and connection afflict the life of vulnerable members of societies. Through the representation of such types of trauma, Gordone attempts to provide the ground for readers and audiences to perceive how the dominant systems of oppression and connection have alienated and denigrated the disempowered members of society. I can say that *No Place to Be Somebody* is at the same time a drama of great force, diligence and commitment and I believe Gabe finds a logical way to voice the concerns of alienated, marginalized, denigrated and disempowered members of society.

Terribly sorry to interrupt. You know, I have to answer the questions. However, later I found that it is not important how good you can answer questions in your defense session, since the grading committee only considers your dissertation! Some of opponents have already written their statements before defense sessions! So what's the philosophy of holding defense sessions!?

Let's get back to our own story until the opponent prepares and poses another question. We got home quickly, took our luggage and headed for the coach terminal. We did buy some foodstuff while waiting for the coach. We did catch coach at 2 pm. We were a bit relieved but still I had some stress. What would happen if the coach runs out of order? Shall we this time ask for reimbursement from coach company? I said reimbursement! We got all documents with ourselves to apply for it when we arrive in our home country. My husband was coughing. He looked pale. He had had lots of distress. Hope he has a speedy recovery. After about two hours, the coach arrived in Vantaa and all of a sudden got stuck in an afternoon traffic! Something we did not expect at all! It was moving like a turtle. Stress was killing me again! I estimated that it will end soon, since we were not far away from the airport. I looked at my watch. It was 4 pm. The speed of the coach was decreasing. There were some flash lights ahead. There were some major road overhaul and repairmen had closed one line of high way.

Soon the couch stopped moving. "What has happened?" was the question of almost all passengers who were heading for the airport. The monitor of the couch was showing the departure flights and ours was on top! But we were not on top. Soon we heard the sirens of a police car, an ambulance and a fire fighting vehicle. I looked at my watch again. It was 4: 35 and wewerestillstuck-inthetrafficjamsinceanaccidenthadhappened. We found it when the road was opened and we passed by two crashed cars. How unlucky we are, I was thinking. We rarely see such scenes in our daily life in Finland but all these happened together to us in one scene. Houno fiilis meillä oli on.[34] The coach speeded up and we arrived at the airport at about 4:50. The coach driver got off first to deliver the luggage. Hurriedly he was throwing all luggage out. It seemed that he himself was late for his next service. I was there to get our luggage and unfortunately he broke the handle of one of our luggage! So far, so good! We only needed this to complete our collection of good events. He changed color out of shame and started to apologize again and again, writing some-thing on a paper, but my ear could hear but nothing. I just put everything on a trolley and ran toward airport departure terminal. Probably the gates are closed by now. Quickly we got to airline check-out desk. There was no one behind the desk. I saw that its staff was is leaving. From far away I shouted, "EXCUSE ME!" She suddenly turned. "We're always in time but this is an excep-tion and we need a novel to explain the reasons of our tardiness!" "But you're late and I can do but nothing for you now!" But how could I explain the whole entire story of our abjection and objec-tion to her at this critical moment? Does it make any difference? Who could understand us and our feelings? All my body got wet and I just sat on the ground. three days and nights I had not slept. My wife tried to raise me but I was discharged. For

Let me add here that in *No Place to Be Somebody* most of the statements about equality and civil rights are relegated to Gabe, who utters long soliloquies in the form of poems, expressing black anger, white oppression and the unequal relationships between whites and blacks.

She was talking to someone on her wireless communication device in Finnish. As soon as she hung up, I heard her say "your passports and tickets please!" What happened? Was she talking to us? My wife hurriedly handed in our passports and tickets. "Put your luggage one by one on scale." They were heavy for me and I looked at my husband. He rose and did the job. The lady returned our passports with some luggage receipts stuck on them. "Gate no. 10," she advised us. We ran toward police inspection gates and then to gate 10. No passenger was in the gate. Immediately we entered the plane and sat on our seats. I was all wet like a drowned rat. Is it over? What's next? An air overhaul? An air accident? Air aground? Air traffic, delay or what? I liked to lis10 to the soft music played in the plane. I didon't want to think about anything else.

The plane took off on time. I could feel my husband's discomfort. He was still sweating and it was impossible for him to change his wet clothes. He looked like a footballer who had run for 120 minutes. We were starving and had our supper eagerly. Everything was moving on smoothly. For the first time in the last three days and nights I was feeling comfortable but as expected this comfort did not last long. The plane started to shudder in the turbulence. Soon the captain started to speak, informing us that one of the engines has stopped working and we should get ready for emergency conditions. The cabin crew themselves looked agitated. I could hear some passengers screaming and some praying. We were flying over Black Sea I suppose. No chance. The trembles and screams were getting more. I knew this might happen. What did I persist too much on this trip? I had to cancel it. This is the end.

In those critical moments I remembered our Flight to Finland. How hapless we were are. Suddenly the passenger sitting next to me frantically threw her purse open, searched searching for a tissue but a violent sneeze ripped through her lungs so quickly that she barely had time to cover her mouth with her hand. Her violent sneeze made me up I get. I looked around and saw that everything is still moving on smoothly. Our tragedy perhaps needed this epilogue, too.

4. Panel Three:

Inadmissible

The First Finnish Immigrant
Happy to hear that you safely arrived home.

The Emigrant
Thanks a billion.

The Finnish Finn
Have you heard what our pääministeri said about immigration?

The Swedish Finn
No. What did he say?

The First Woman Voter
He said he feels Finland should set an example to the rest of Europe on immigration. I suppose we can. We were the first in Europe to give the right of vote to women. We can also become no. 1 in creating equal opportunity for all people legally residing in Finland, regardless of their color, race, gender, name, belief and religion.

King Charles Frederick
I'm also an immigrant but a privilegiert one, more privilegiert than you.

The First Finnish Immigrant
This is the way toward progress, I mean equality.

The Veteran
I also think if we do not take acsion to build a united strong nasion based on equality and meritocracy, we will continue to have

many alien nasions within our nasion. The result is frustrasion and despair. I believ our pääministeri knows what he says. He sees the future. We sould trust him.

The Emigrant
Do you mean I can get fund and job without a need to change my moniker?

The Finnish Refugee
I'm not sure. Try both ways.

The Swedish Finn
The best equation of liv is to build a bridge over the lake of despair. HOPE stands for Hold On! Problems End.

The Gabe Gabriel
Racial discrimination plays out in job searches for our candidates even dose who hold degrees from elite schools. Der are disparities in both deh number of responses black and white job candidates receive from employers and in deh level of starting salaries offered.

The Emigrant
Invisible barbed wires always are.

The Meta-Medium
Good evening! Our top 10 stories tonight: The Finnish Security Intelligence Service says that more than 70 people have left Finland to join the extremist groups. The security police estimate that two thirds of them are Finnish citizens. FSIS says that the phenomenon peaked a year ago, but that there are no signs that the flow of individuals is drying up. FSIS officials also said that the flow began two years ago and has led to a raised terrorism threat in Finland since last summer. Some of those who have gone to join radicalism had no previous involvement with any religion and had never even been in religious centers before leaving Finland. About half have lived their whole lives in Finland. Finland is concerned about the possible threat of blowback

from its nationals who return home. They estimate that about 20 nationals have already returned to Finland.

The Police Wo-Man
O my gosh! Turn it of. I don't wanna here tis.

The Finnish Finn
Some of them have returned and are living with us? Oh my goodness! Why they join extremists?

The First Finnish Immigrant
I was treated unfairly when immigrated to the New World. Discrimination kills. Connection kills. Lack of connection kills, too.

The Swedish Finn
We should do whatever we can to stop this trend.

The Meta-Medium
Brea-king of b-reaking news: The Minister for Foreign Affairs revealed in an interview just a second ago that a proportionally large number of people have left Finland to fight for extremist groups. He noted that the number of Finns who have left the country to join the ranks of extremist groups currently stands at approximately 100 and that roughly 20 of them have been killed.

The Police Wo-Man
Shut it dawn. Its breaking newz is reali bricking me.

The Emigrant
No worries! We can easily solve the problem.

The Police Wo-Man
How?

The Emigrant
Send them to insurance companies.

The Police Wo-Man
Do not let your cence of violet humor leak. I jug you otherwise.

The Swedish Finn
But it does not change anything. We should find a proper way out of this crisis. As we have heralded in many good issues in the world, we can be and continue to be a nation without nations, a nation without alien|nations I mean.

The Police Wo-Man
Stop filosofizing and shut it dawn I said. Its breaking newz is reali bricking me. Do you under stand me?

The Emigrant
I was just reading the website of Finland Ministry of the Interior website. It states that "Finland is an open and safe country" and explains the country's policy toward migration. Let me read it for you:

> The Strategy views migration as an opportunity: mobility creates international networks and brings with it new ways of doing things. Migration will help to answer Finland's dependency ratio problem, but at the same time, competition for workers between countries will increase. To succeed in this competition, Finland must be able to effectively attract *skilled workers* who will stay in the country for the longer term. As a responsible member of the international community, Finland is committed to providing international protection to those who need it.

The ministry also adds that "everyone can find a role to play," and "diversity is part of everyday life."

The Finnish Finn
The Swedish Finn
The First Woman Voter
The First Finnish Immigrant
The Veteran
The Police Wo-Man

The Emigrant
The Finnish Refugee
The Gabe Gabriel
King Charles Frederick

The Emigrant

Just you need *skilled workers*?! As Max Frisch says, "We asked for *workers*. We got *people* instead." Don't you need scientists, scholars, specialists, sportsmen, investors, inventors, researchers, managers?

The First Finnish Immigrant

Nice motto! A question to understand the role of immigrants in this country: what would happen if one day all immigrants in Finland decide to go on a strike?

The Finnish Finn

We don't need vain workers. It's not fair to have aliens just as workers. To me, they can also become bus drivers. Aliens make really nice bus drivers here, don't they? They are polite and do not even look at your ticket.

The Emigrant

Like any other countries, there are great things and not-so-great things. I was in a camp for about a year filing an application for refugee status in Europe. My application was successful but I was told that I have to go to Finland. "Finland?" I was expected to go to Germany, Sweden or England. I was so depressed, since Finland due to its cold weather and its lack of internationality didon't look like a haven for aliens. As Tony Blur said, "A simple way to take measure of a country is to look at how many want in . . . and how many want out." But no choice! If I declined, my application would be declared null and void. But now I feel I love it here. I love the simplicity of life, its pure nature, cleanliness, etc. Even now when I travel to other countries such as Germany, Sweden and England I miss Finland, its peace and quietness. One of the main problems here for aliens is job discrimination. First you are told that you need to master the language to get a job and after you master the language you won't get any job. Job discrimination has badly affected the lives of aliens. Then desperately you at10d some technical courses and become either a driver or a barber or a pizzeria 10der and if you are a woman, you become either a janitor, a hairdresser or a caregiver in nursing homes to take care of elders that every day nag that they don't want an alien to push their wheelchairs around. And you always receive the hardest shifts in your work. After lots of challenges, I was hired as a bus driver but after a year municipality ended its contract with company I was working for due to the poor conditions of its buses and I lost my job. After a year or so I'm still jobless. Joblessness syphons your energy away and do you know what the quickest way to die is? USE-LESSNESS. I have come here to give something to society and not just receive from it but even our second generation that have raised here and have university degrees are unable to get jobs in governmental offices.

The Finnish Finn
The Swedish Finn
The First Woman Voter
The First Finnish Immigrant
The Veteran
The Police Wo-Man
The Finnish Refugee
The Gabe Gabriel
King Charles Frederick

The Emigrant
I'm coming from a country in which helping others is a virtue and my countrymen do it willingly as soon as they feel you need help. When they themselves see or feel that you need help, they stretch their hands. Here people see that I need help but who cares! Some weeks ago my colleague also an alien told me that he never helps anyone in Finland. When I asked him about the reason, he said that he tried to help a Finnish lady but she got furious claiming, "Do you feel I'm weaker than you? Here is Finland not your homeland! Women are as strong as men. You'd

better know it if you didon't." I wish people here were not as distant as they are. A short greeting or a smile do not cost anything for us but can make days more awesome.

The First Finnish Immigrant
Since my arrival I have miss smile. I miss saying hello to my neighbors. I thought if I buy a house my condition would improve and could build up a nice relationship with my neighbors but it was not rite. When I pass my neighbors in streets they ignore me unless I force them and catch their eyes and say HELLO first. Then they might nod. Do you believe me that I have never been able to have a chat with my next door old neighbor since my arrival?! I don't know his first name yet and he doesn't know mine.

The Finnish Finn
It seems that being far away from Finland has made you forget all about here. Why should we greet our neighbors? No need. And why should we know the first name of our neighbor? The less you know, the better you live. SO FAR, SO GOOD! Isn't it better? Some time ago while I was in a bus stop waiting for bus my colleague stopped his car and offered me a ride to our workplace but I declined. Why should he stop his car for a lady? Since then I am afraid of him. What was his intention? What does he think of me now?

The Emigrant
What?! You live in a beautiful country and have nothing to complain about. You need to cheer up, live your life, enjoy every moment of it, smile and help each other, remove the distance and bring down high suicide rate.

The Finnish Finn
_____KKK.

The Gabe Gabriel
I have been looking for uh job in Finland since I arrived here and no one has ever uhnswered my emails or phone calls tuh say why

I didn't get dat job. And when ya're driving at deh speed limit you will be overtaken by some Finnish drivers constantly. Some travel guide books call Finns calm but dey are uhlways in hurry while driving. Talking on deir mobile phones while driving is uhlso common and not uh problem at uhll!

The Finnish Finn
As for using mobile phone while driving you might not know that Finns are professional drivers? We can even text while driving. So that's not a problem at all.

The Police Wo-Man
Who usez sell fone while driving?! Just show them to me. I'm hear to fine them! Hear is Fineland.

The First Finnish Immigrant
I changed my name to Pehr Kalm and swam a lot in Niagara.

The Finnish Finn
I have read your book but had no chance to meet you. Nice to meet you here in this noveramatry.

The Swedish Finn
I've read your book too. Good job fellow.

The First Finnish Immigrant
Good to hear that. I forgot to write in my book that I brought with myself to the US some types of grains such as rye, barely and oat and for a while I worked there as a farmer. But then drought and lack of water made me work as a domestic worker. Then the situation got better and I became Emil Hurja.

The Finnish Finn
Really surprised to hear about your adventures.

The Swedish Finn
What a complicated life you've had.

The Swedish Finn
The Finnish Finn

The Finnish Finn
The Swedish Finn

The Finnish Finn
We are proud of you, Emil.

The Swedish Finn
I've heard about you, Man.

The Emigrant
I suppose some immigrants act like rye, barley and oat. They grow when they are buried. They become flour when they are ground under stones of discriminations, inequality and injustices. They change to bread when they are burnt burned and they nourish when they are bitten, but note that some might not.

King Charles Frederick
If I would choose to be your könig, I would bring some noble blut to rule here, NOT skilled workers. Then you could see the key rolle of immigrants in Finnland.

The Gabe Gabriel
Uhny immigrant wid Finnish citizenship in deh parliament or ministries or governmental offices?

The Emigrant
Good question.

The Meta-Medium
Good evening. Bruise today: Finland has a population of about 300,000 of foreign origin, which is 5.5% of the total population. Over the last 10 years, this number has increased by about 20,000 per year while at the same time there has been no recognizable change in the country's immigration policies. If immigration continues with similar or higher numbers, it is clear that Finland will not be able to successfully integrate these populations and guarantee the main10ance of societal peace in the country.

The First Woman Voter
This means frustration, violence, crisis, protest. This brings social, economic and political crises.

The Swedish Finn
Reverse emigration probably. Cloud seeding ceding I mean.

The Chorus

We hereby maintain that there is only one race and that is human race. We can live together in peace despite our differences. We can be like leaves of different trees, trees of different species, trees of different colors to make a nice forest together. The leaves of grass of different types, colors and sizes. Let's sing a song:

Human beings are members of a whole,

 In creation of one essence and soul.

  If one member is afflicted with pain,

   Other members uneasy will remain.

    If you've no sympathy for human pain,

     The name of human you cannot retain![35]

3. Season One:

A Man who Chose to Live

I love this poem and every now and then I read it not to forget who I am. Anyway, we had a nice journey home, happy holidays and reunion which made us forget about all our trip miseries. We also scanned and submitted our documents for reimbursement to Viking Line and they nicely took care of it. Just in a few days they informed me that they had have transferred the money to my account. However, the reimbursement later created a tax problem for me, receiving a mail from tax office saying that I have to pay some tax on the received money. But that was not a new income, so why should I pay tax for it? I visited tax office, crowded as usual. My turn after an hour. To get sure that I've properly understood con10t of the letter, I first asked tax officer to explain it to me. Yes, I had got it right. Then I explained everything but she was not receptive, repeating that you've earned this money and according to law you have to pay tax for it! "I had not earned it, it's my own money returned to me after all; it's reimbursement, neither salary nor income nor wage." Then she called someone, perhaps her supervisor and talked to him in Finnish. It seemed that she is giving him a report rather than asking a question. Right after hanging up, she told me that I have to pay tax for the earned money. But that was not fair! "May I talk to your supervisor?" She was reluctant but after a moment of indecision dialed a number and gave me the receiver. I explained everything to her supervisor. "Now I understand," he said, "no problem. No need to pay tax for it." Three telegraphic sen10ces which saved my soul that day. Then he asked her colleague on the phone to correct my earning information in their system.

My coughs were with me and had become even worse. I should visit a doctor when I'm back to Finland, I was determined. On our way to airport, our taxi driver was curious to learn about our destination.

جواب دادیم فنلاند و وی گفت:"شنیدم فنلاند خیلی عالی است. کشورهای دور و برش مثل سنگاپور و اندونزی و مالزی هم عالی هستن."

و ما با تعجب گفتیم: "چی؟ سنگاپور، اندونزی و مالزی؟! اما فنلاند در شمال اروپاست!" با این سطح عالی از معلومات جغرافیا خوشحال شدیم که به جای فرودگاه ما را به قبرستان نبرد.[36]

By this time, I had also made my mind to change my supervisors and even my department. I could not bear and grin it anymore. One of them was killing me with his ill-treatments. My sisu was over and I was determined to move. Several other PhD students had left were are leaving that department and even Finland. Just few students had managed to finish their PhD studies in the history of that department, less than the number of fingers of one hand. Do you believe me that just right now that I am writing this work, a PhD student is desperately leaving that department? By that time, I had writ10 three chapters of my dissertation and discussed them with my supervisors and even presented them in our departmental seminars and international conferences.

I had two main reasons to move: One he did not lis10 to me at all. For instance, when we got together to discuss a chapter, he asked what do you mean by this sentence, sometimes with a sneer and before I open my mouth to explain or just after a few words uttered, she restlessly interrupted me saying, "I don't understand what you mean meant. Cut this part." There were some reasons behind those ideas but he was reluctant to lis10 at all, and in a couple of times that I insisted to explain what I mean meant she got irritated. So I had to delete my ideas just because he had no interest to lis10 to my reasons.

Two, she refused to write recommendation letters under different pretexts whenever an opportunity arose. For instance, once I saw a notice at university that EU dispatches some PhD students for a month to Canada to visit different Canadian universities and connects them with their concerned departments. That was a fully-funded project. Immediately I contacted those people in Brussels. They reviewed my conditions and informed me that there is a quota for each country, including Finland, which has not been fully filled yet and in case I apply for that I have a high chance. They also asked me to send my documents along with a reference letter. I contacted my supervisor, explained everything and asked for his reference letter. I even assured him that this visit –

based on my inquiries from the trip organizers – will give me the possibility to at10d some courses on African American literature and meet with some scholars in my own field of research during my trip. She replied "NO" as expected.

The Gabe Gabriel
African American uhgain!!! American literature.

It was senseless to argue with her. That was his outworn strategy. He always said "NO" to skip her responsibility. Even to fill in her own online duty tables on monthly basis made her irritated. My past experience showed that if I argue with her, he retorts, "You'd better finnish writing your dissertation first and we can decide later about such trips." If I asked for recommendation to apply for some fund, either he refused to reply my emails or said, "this foundation is not proper for humanities and there are some better ones coming up soon! So you'd better be patient." When I had just started my work under her supervision, I was naïve and easily bamboozled by such statements but later this way looked tattered and torn to me. I hope she was more "creative" and could devise some novel ways! As for foundations that he claimed were "improper" for humanities as he claimed, some of my colleagues at the Faculty of Humanities applied and even received it. Once my colleagues were shocked to hear about my claim that this is not for humanities; they opened website of that foundation and showed me exactly where it noted the areas of applications, including humanities, but who dared to tell him so! I also preferred not to talk about my concern with my colleagues at our department, since I thought it would not help, so I just tried to be patient and suppress my feelings. Sometimes they asked me why I didon't apply for some foundation that welcome welcomed applications and I had nothing to say. He had another outworn strategy to skip her responsibility: to postpone my applications. He sometimes mentioned the names of some foundations which didon't exist at all and if existed they were are not intended for such a purpose. In one case, surfing the net for hours showed that the foundation that he mentioned will welcome application soon was active for research on Parkinson and Alzheimer treatments!

I was studying African American literature, seeing how they resisted against injustice, racism, inequality and discrimination and how I could see the negligence of my rights. I had to take action. I did whatever I could to change her behaviors toward myself believing that time heals all sorrows but time failed to heal my sorrows. She continued her nasty behaviors towards me making me believe that it's really harder than you think and even impossible to change some people. To me, such people are like a baked clay urn. They have badly formed and any attempt to change them might break them and cut your hands. He once clearly told me that she prefers to write recommendations for his Finnish students. Is it a type of racism or not? What do you think?

But he had devoted all her life to the study of racism, classism, sexism, etc. He has writ10 some papers on racism, classism and sexism, so how could she act like that? And more importantly, he had no Finnish students; they had already left or graduated. To me those two students who had graduated under his supervision were really resistant, enlivening sisu in a real sense. In his dissertation acknowledgements, one of those students had noted that he also wanted to leave thanking another colleague who helped her persist and resist!

However, this figure on a couple of occasions in three and half years became different. He did give me some Easter eggs on Easter or some books for the New Year to my daughter or suddenly opened his heart to me, talking about everything for hours and I lis10ed at10tively while asking myself whether she is the same person? What has happened? Is she drunk or what? Has she dreamed a horrible dream about what he has done to me during all these years, and that has changed her? I did not believe my eyes. But this did not last for more than a few hours. Once when he was in such a nice mood, I got dared to ask her for a recommendation letter; my heart panted, thinking that this request would ruin our sweet conversation that has happened after some years full of 10sion but to my surprise she said, "Sure, my pleasure! You've worked really hard during these years and I'm fully satisfied with your progress." That application, however, was not successful! Two extremes this time in one person! She "granted" me many sleepless nights with her maltreatments. Let bygones be bygones! I'm defending and this journey with lots of ups and downs is coming to an end after all. Let me cheer up.

I had two ways: either to leave Finland like some other doctoral candidates in that department or to change my university. I went for the latter because I had studied hard during all those years and had written a major part of my dissertation. In addition, too much leaving is a dangerous thing, isn't it? Väinämöinen also left Finland, declaring that someday his services will be in great demand. I went for the latter. I decided to divorce him for religious reasons: He thought He was God and I was His servant. By the way, do you know what's the main reason for divorce?[37] Any idea? Write it here:

I started my negotiations with another professor in another university, and he was quite receptive. The application process started. Some forms to fill in, some documents to hand in, some petitions to write down and more importantly some decisions to be made. When handed in the required documents, I learned that Faculty meeting is held once a month and the most recent one was just today morn. "So the next meeting of the Faculty is next month," our postgraduate coordinator advised me. Anxiety again. Another gnikcuf A . A stressful and tough month passed but to me each day was as looooooooooooooooooooooooooooooooong as a year. Thankfully the decision was positive and I found a new home, two supportive and lovely supervisors with a great sense of understanding, commitment, expertise and experience. It was worth moving. I was quite happy with the result. My agitation, my despair, my internal conflict, my frustration were all over. My family also relieved. We no longer needed need to talk about such issues at home. Have you heard "sweat today for sweet to-morrow?" My supervisors lis10ed at10tively and thoughtfully commented which helped me improve my work. This was what I desired. I didon't need to delete whatever seemed vague to them; rather I had an opportunity to discuss my ideas. They patiently lis10ed to me and I had the opportunity to defend my views. Two extremes again! The world abounds with many extremes. Any other extremes or binary oppositions do you have in mind or ex-perienced in your life? List them below:

Despite all her maltreatments toward me, I still feel indebted to my ex-supervisor. I believe we should build walls with other people's goodness and if they were unkind to us we should take only one of bricks away and not to break down the whole wall.

Why have you seen Gabe Gabriel and Johnny Rome'o as a binary opposition in you' disse'tation?

In my view, these are two characters with two different strategies and viewpoints to cope with alienation and exile. Gabe advocates literacy and literature and looks into the future with optimism rather than highlighting the wrongs of the past. To me, he represents the Old Negro that favors moral debate whereas Johnny stands for the New Negro, I mean a postwar generation undaunted by the possibility that militant action serves a central role in black political and personal self-actualization. He is full of rage of rejection and ejection and to achieve power and affluence as tokens of success he looks after physical superiority. Gabe also looks for power and place but he opposes the adoption of wrong values of the white community. So as I said he desires to succeed as a writer and actor in the white world. He who signifies the angel in the Abrahamic religions takes this to fight against invisibility and inaudibility, anonymity and alienation.

The Gabe Gabriel

Negro?! uld Negro?! New Negro?! Ya'r defendin' in 21st century Man. Stop usin' such out-worn terms!

Thanks to my supervisors. They supported me to have a visiting research position at Lakehead University, Thunder Bay, Canada, and since it was for two months my husband and daughter accompanied me. There were so many geographical similarities between town we live in Finland and Thunder Bay. My husband

117

and I were at the university and its main library, doing our own research. Thunder Bay had about 120,000 residents and around 30,000 were people of Finnish backgrounds, meaning out of four people you met meet, one was Finnish and three others have had been affected by Finns; either married to a Finn or had a Finnish neighbor or colleague. There I met with a Finnish professor from history department who was the head of Finlandia, Finnish cultural association in that town. He kindly introduced me to some librarians and asked them to give me some access to their great archives and sources on Finns and their history of immigration to Canada, great archives and sources that have not received the at10tion they really deserve.

I was am having a meeting with my supervisors tomorrowyestertoday about the defense session and they brief briefed me about the formalities of the defense session. I've been to some of defense sessions in the past and familiarized myself with its so many dos and don'ts that I must observe. I'm quite familiar with them by now. We also need to agree on a dress code, either a black tailcoat or black suit and white shirt. I am for black suit and white shirt, but let's see.

The Gabe Gabriel
I love it Man. Black is deh color of formality and is foregrounded. In addition, white and black gaw tuhgeder quite well.

The Emigrant
Yes, I do agree with you. Black and white can go together nicely.

You must also learn how to enter the lecture hall. The defender first, followed by custos and opponent in a row, who begins who continues how to say what to say when to sit where to sit when to rise who will conclude how to answer the questions and dispute, to name but a few. I've already done good, except I was a bit fast when we entered the lecture hall, I was excited and like a rabbit jumped on stage while my custos and opponent were far behind. I couldn't see behind my back and thus I failed to set my pace with them!

Before our departure, we rented a house in Bay Street, a street known for its great number of Finnish population. We rented the second floor of a house, owned by a kind old lady, originally from Sweden, born to Swedish immigrant parents in Thunder Bay. Although she was on a wheelchair, she could drive her huge American car professionally. Every morning, she got up early and had her breakfast with ABA. She then had her lunch with BCB and her supper with CDC and slept with ABA. When heard that we have already traveled to more than 20 countries she envied us confessing that she has had only visited some parts of Canada and some of the nearby US cities and sees the world via these Tea Vea channels!

The Finnish Finn
The Swedish Finn
The First Woman Voter
The First Finnish Immigrant
The Veteran

The Police Wo-Man
The Emigrant
The Finnish Refugee
The Gabe Gabriel
King Charles Frederick

When I was telling her about Finland, its high level of welfare, its safety and its nice cultural and socio-economic systems, she was looking at me with doubt and then she said that Finland might be good but it cannot be compared with Canada. She referred me to Anthony Bourdain's documentary on CNN about Finland and said that she could not watch more than 10 minutes of that because it was awful! It was hard or rather impossible to clear images she had seen in that "documentary." As the last resort, I invited her to Finland so as to see here with her own eyes rather than from the lens of Tea Vea.

Finnish flags are were everywhere in Bay Street; Muumi dolls, Fazer chocolates, Finnish books and Finnish local newspapers are were seen everywhere. So we spoke Finnish more than English in that street, in its shops, cultural association, restaurants and coffee shops. When we had just arrived, we met a group of elders sitting in front of Ravintola Hoito. I greeted them saying, "Moi" but they did not reply. Later I found that they do not understand what Moi means meant; rather they use used "Terrrve." Finns that we met there had a lot to share with us about their immigration experiences, life in Canada, their children, their opinions of Finland, their customs and activities.

To be sure that we get to the university on time, we always departed home earlier because we always knew we meet some neighbors who were either watering their gardens or mowing their lawn or walking their dogs on the way and they always know how to start a lovely conversation and how to continue it for hours! Many of them asked us with a sense of humor how we have survived in Finland, telling us that when after years they visit visited their relatives in Finland they are were shocked with their cultural differences! An old couple told us that they had have just returned from Finland but each time they visit their homeland they feel less Finnish! Most Finns, they believed, have a coldly reserved outside face shown to strangers and a warmly reserved inside face used with their family and very close friends. They added that it's cultural but that doesn't make it any less frustrating for someone visiting from another place where acts of assistance and smiling are common. "It's not a chore to smile with sincerity and wish a stranger you pass on a morning walk 'a good day.' It makes us happy to be helpful or acknowledge something someone didos but didoesn't have to do because we are all human-*kind*," they maintained. "We should not be afraid of people who smile; it's horrible that displays of happiness are considered a sign of mental problem! Smile is not the sign of weakness, it's a sign of peace!" Two extremes again! Upon hearing their words, I thought I've traumatized some people here in Finland with my smiles, greetings and offers of help.

There were are held some Finnish courses for people who were are interested in Thunder Bay but teachers complained that the second and third generations of Finnish immigrants do not show much interest to acquire their mother tongue.

Let me say that I won't be available for a few days. I've received some comments from a journal on a paper of mine, so I have to apply those comments, revise and resubmit the paper. I'll get back to you pretty fast. Please take some deep breaths.

2. Panel Four:

This is not to be Desert we Inhibit

The Gabe Gabriel
Didya revise and resubmit yor paper?

The Emigrant
Yes.

The Finnish Finn
Good luck!

The Swedish Finn
Great! Let's smile. Did you hear what our fellow countryman who resides in Canada say?

The Finnish Finn
Yes but I can't smile artificially at all times. That will bring wrinkles around my eyes. I hate wrinkles.

The Gabe Gabriel
Ya duhn't need tuh smile artificially. Ya kin practice tuh smile naturally. I take uh cold shower and join ya soon.. I kin't stand dat amount of heat.

The Emigrant
Me too. I come with you.

The Meta-Medium
Studies suggest that smiling either forced or choiced can have a positive effect on man's well-being. It decreases stress level and impresses people around you positively. Lots of people spend

thousands of euros every year to boost their health conditions. Scientists have found that there are other ways they can boost their health conditions, mood and longevity for free. One of the easiest ways is to smile. Scientists have also discovered that smiling increases productivity, enhances at10tion and trust of other people toward you, builds attraction and boosts your immune system. Scientists also found that people who are physically unable to smile suffer from *moebius syndrome*.

The Swedish Finn
I can smile. I have not syndrome of any type.

The Veteran
I can smile too. Look at meeee!

The Finnish Refugee
Let me try_____. It's hard. Could me? Do you trust me now?

The Police Wo-Man
I love to smil but if I do no one iz afraid of me. I like to be frai10ing. Frai10ing bringz atrakshion to me. Smil killz atrakshion. I don't need other people's trust. I have uniform. That's enuf.

The Emigrant
-K, but at least smile when you are alone with your colleagues in your coffee room or after sending people to insurance companies.

The Swedish Finn
Do you know that election is next month?

The First Woman Voter
Yes I see election campaigns all over the country. I love it. This is what I have struggled for.

The Gabe Gabriel
How many political parties are active in Finland?

The Finnish Finn
Let's say NINE.

The Gabe Gabriel
Nine for 5500000 is perfect. We have only two for 333000000!

The Emigrants
If we form one, we will hit 10. But it is prior for us to vote first, to know that voting is our responsibility, to coalesce and vote for some candidates who will defend aliens' neglected rights after they enter the parliament.

The Swedish Finn
I'm concerned about the growth of a right-wing party which politely says, "Aliens! Get lost." But they can't say it like that because they hate to speak English. They even refuse refused to sign an anti-racism appeal and agree agreed with a statement declaring "People of certain races are unsuited for life in Finland!"

The First Finnish Immigrant
We published many newspapers and many cultural foundations. Please visit our Knights of Kaleva and Order of Runeberg and Finlandia. Lots of programs we have for you. Also read *Raivaaja* and *New Yorkin Uutiset* if you have time. There we formed some campaigns complaining why Americans didn't truly understand the significance of Finnish immigrants. We were a minority group but deserved much more at10tion.

The Gabe Gabriel
But dis- is in sharp contrast with deh country's policy tuhward immigration! Uh number of Finns favor and back dis- party and vote for it, meaning dey dislike immigrants, while deh government's Strategy views immigration as an opportunity! On deh oder side, they claim dat dey are not racists, so how uh great number of dem vote for dat party? Weird! But as Allen west truly says, "now is an opportunity for us to stand up and have a good, strong immigration policy."

The Finnish Finn
The Swedish Finn
The First Woman Voter
The First Finnish Immigrant
The Veteran
The Police Wo-Man
The Finnish Refugee
King Charles Frederick

The Emigrant
_____this is threa10ing! Many of its supporters are employers, authorities in different sections, decision makers in public and private enterprises and you see how they can turn the page against aliens' applications in everything, employment, grant, etc.

The Swedish Finn
These are populists. They know how to play tight and loose with grassroots' emotion. They are as a magnat attracting loose nails. Now anti-immigration mottos are in vogue and they form anti-immigration campaigns but after they win people's vote they forget about what they chanted! Political parter take power but not many changes happen in laws. What have they done?! What can they do? Nothing just wordnotwork.

Do you want to know what new laws or modifications are passed and enacted in the future?

The Emigrant
Yes, I'm curious.

So keep an eye on Sweden parliament. We are wise. We look at laws enacted by the Riksdag. After their trial and error, we go to the edge of our understanding whether those laws work for us too? If they have desired results and effects, we implement them as well.

The Emigrant
Hahahahahaha. Finns are wise.

The Chorus
Aliens should write to right,
> should claim for their aim,
>> should fight for their right.
>>> If not fight, they should flight.

The Emigrant
Where is The Police Wo-Man? I don't see herim.

The Police Wo-Man
I'm just hear. I needed a drink. Did you miss me? What's rong again?

The Emigrant
Why the police gates at airports are divided into two: one for EU|EEA Nationals and one for Non-EU|EEA Nationals? Why not only one type of gate for all?

The Police Wo-Man
No idea, probably a teknikal ishu. Why do you wana chalenge everything? I'll jug you huh!

The Emigrant
Just a question it was is being. We should vote as we should write as responsible members of this society. Let's not be in the state of hibernation. We are not Jack-the-Bear. We should not occupy a space without use. So come on! We are the dynamo of energy. V and W = V

The Chorus
V + W = V | W + V = V | V = W + V | V = V + W

The Meta-Medium
Studies show that smiling even a forced one can have a positive effect on your well-being. It decreases your stress level and even

impresses people around you positively. Scientists found that people who are physically unable to smile suffer from *moebius syndrome* and they need to visit a psychologist. They not only damage their own health but also damage the mood of their colleagues, friends and neighbors. Their research also revealed that lots of people spend thousands of euros every year to boost their health conditions. Scientists have found that there are other ways they can boost their health conditions, mood and longevity for free. One of the easiest ways is to smile. Scientists have also discovered that smiling boosts your immune system, builds attraction, increases productivity and enhances at10tion and trust of other people toward you.

The Gabe Gabriel
Let's smile and leave deh sauna. Dat was uh great experience for me. We kin continue our chat in deh common room while having some coffee. I feel really relaxed.

Please devise some dialogues, monologues, songs or anything that you wish to finnish the play:

1. Reseason Four:

I Look Upward and See the Summit

My wife and I usually had our lunch together in front of a lake at Lakehead University if the weather was nice or if she did not have some experiments to do. That means we rarely had lunch together, because either the weather was awful or she had some experiments to do! Once when the weather was nice but my wife was engaged with a number of successive experiments, I borrowed a book from university main library and walked out to enjoy reading in the nice weather. I saw a man with a dark skin gazing at lake. No one was around and when on the way I got closer to him, he suddenly looked up and we both smiled. That smile was enough to tie our hearts together. At first he looked worried to open his heart to me but when he found that I'm coming for a visiting research from Finland, he found me a reliable ear. So every now and then we met in campus or library and talked about their historical discriminations and oppressions that have lasted so far.

In fact, he was an Aboriginal. He told me how whites have always neglected and restricted their rights which is an expression of their racist attitudes and policies directed at Aboriginals, told me how many of his people commit committed suicide as a result of such policies and attitudes, told me how some of them resort resorted to alcohol or marijuana to escape their sufferings, told me how their lives have been destroyed and are still, told me that some Aboriginal Studies Departments at Canadian universities have been established but have all been occupied by whites and there is not even an aboriginal staff among them and they have right to write whatever they wish on their behalf and represent them in any way they desire, told me how they call us lazy bones and good-for-nothing just to continue putting them down, told me how the prospects for Aboriginal employment were are dismal and how and how and how. He noted that the rate of unemployment for Aboriginals is 10 times higher than that recorded for non-Aboriginals. This is awful, isn't it?

The Gabe Gabriel
For us uhlso deh unemployment rate is much higher. It's 30 percent for us while it's only 5 percent for dem. We uhlso refuse tuh send any pic wid our job applications. We also suffer from drug abuse, police brutality, suicide and uh lot more. Ya know, der are many open wounds in our community dat have not healed yet. Like ya we have many challenges Man.

The Emigrant
I see.

"The paradox is that they call us 'First' Nation but in fact we are Last Nation," he continued. "Aboriginal people have a long and proud history, rich cultural and spiritual traditions but many of our traditions have been altered or even taken away by whites upon their arrival. They usurped our traditions like the way they

130

usurped our lands and forced their cultural values to us. Just spend a night with us and see with your own eyes what I say. Come and see what poverty, poor education and discriminations have done to our mental and physical health and identity. But who cares?_____ We are getting exterminated."

He told me that he is 35 years old, and in his lifetime especially after his father committed suicide he has had any type of lowest paying jobs you could imagine just to support himself and his family. "I can never forget my father's body when I found him hanging from the gallows and that image has haunted me hunted always all ways."

The Gabe Gabriel

Hhhow hhhorrible. Hhhoow terrible. Hhhooww traumatic. I've never seen my dad. Have I had one at all? How didoes he look like? My mom uhlso has no idea who he was. Weird, isn't it? By deh way, I was ulienated from deh dominantly white community as well. I did my best tuh be somebody but deh society rejected me.

While writing this paragraph, I looked up and saw a man with black suit and tie at university campus and gazed at him like the way I was gazed at while I had suit and tie in the street, remember? No in10tion I had to gaze at him. He just looked handsome. Perhaps people who gazed at me on that day had no in10tion at all.

He viewed whites with distrust, anger and resentment, telling me that "they view us as savage, barbarian and inferior." He had just been admitted to Lakehead University as a result of the support of some Aboriginals who immigrated to some other countries and made a better life for themselves and now they have decided to open a foundation in order to support some talented students from their original hometown and he is one of them, so they pay for his tuition fees but he still needs to work so as to support his family. He said that there are now some Aboriginal artists, activists and scholars that are working to challenge the status of Aboriginal peoples but we are just at the beginning of the road.

The Gabe Gabriel
Kin Aboriginals and African Americans and immigrants defend uh democracy dat has denied dem and deir rights? We have done it at different occasions but it didn't change anything.

The Emigrant
"African American" you said?! Say American please hereafter.

The Gabe Gabriel
Ohhhhhhhh. A goof I made!

I loved his diligence. I enjoyed lis10ing to him and his determination to struggle his dark past. He had noveramatries to recount, noveramatries that could set fire to readers, noveramatries that have had have the power to move a body to tear and to rage. I suggested him to write down his fiery narratives which burn which awaken which open up. I told him of African Americans and their struggles toward equality. I told him about Du Bois's idea of Talented 10th. He loved the idea and promised to write as soon as he can. I could see hope in his brown eyes, a determina-

132

tion to improve their lives while rediscovering their traditional and cultural values after years of oppression. On the last day I hugged him and reminded him of his promise. He nodded while tears rolling down his cheeks.

The Gabe Gabriel
Even though we have long claimed American identities, we have not been accepted as full citizens yet and have been discriminated uhgainst. So like ya, we have been part of America but still outside it. Dis- is deh case for our literature. As ya know, I've produced some works but dey exist not fully widin deh framework of American literature. Don't ya see dat deh disputant still uses "African American" in his lectio and defense and refuses tuh correct himself? As uh mulatto and as uhlways labeled African American, I myself suffer from two-ness, uh duality. I am both an American and African, both uh white and black; I have two souls, two thoughts uhll and uhll in one body, two cultures sometimes in clash, and even two homes.

How could we live in Finland and do not learn Finnish? That's not fair. We at10ded some Finnish courses in the meantime. Our Finnish teachers all ladies were exemplary, patient and committed. We loved them a lot but not their piles of homework. But love me love my dog|doll? We had to spend a lot of time and energy on Finnish homework. The more we study studied and the more we sweat sweated, the less we learned learnt learn! There was nothing wrong with our teachers but with the system I suppose. First they teach you grammar grammaar grammaarr. Then they spend lots of time and energy to teach you writing skills. Once and after a couple of years that you learn those skills, they tell you that we do not speak as such! The course is over.

133

Näkemiin! As a result of such a system, one year after at10ding several courses and doing tons of homework, you realize that your Finnish skills are that hi that you begin with "hei" and ends with "hei hei" while you are unable to say anything in-between. In the second year, you start with "hei," continue by asking addressee "puhutko englantia?" and elegantly end with "hei hei" or "kiitos ja hei." And in the third year, you utter some more sen10ces in Finnish but when addressee answers or asks a question, you understand that you have understood but nothing and then ask them again "puhutko englantia?"

The First Finnish Immigrant
This reminds me of evening English language courses we had to at10d. We were tired, dead tired after 10 hours of daily work but had to at10d those courses to acquire citizenship. Tons of homework we also received. The English examination for citizenship was one of the most stressful and frigh10ing event in our life. History mystery! But do I speak English fluently now? Do you like my American accent?

The Emigrant
I love your accent. What a similarity! YKI test is also stressful and frigh10ing for immigrants here.

The First Finnish Immigrant
I practiced a lot as I wanted to remove any signs of Finnishness even in my accent. That helped me a lot to assimilate.

The Emigrant
I understand.

Last week after my defense, we had lunch with our nice Finnish teacher and her husband. We had a nice chat for about two hours just in Finnish! They spoke Finnish and we spoke Finiglidsh. Nice progress! We have problems only in endings and vocabularies and grammar and pronunciations. That's all. I can speak and write Finnish now like The Police Wo-Man speaking and writing English. I had another teacher, a young lady, who was always smiling and I wondered whether her cheeks actually do not hurt from smiling all day? An answer to those who believe Finns do not smile! Take it. One of our Finnish teachers urged us to speak Finnish wherever we go, emphasizing that it speeds up our learning process, no matter what happens. I was determined to follow her instruction. Tomorrow we were going to football stadium. During halftime, my daughter asked for some refreshments. It was our turn after all. I ordered in Finnish: "Kaks jäätelöä."[38] But before my sen10ce ends, seller asked, "Do you want your ice-creams in cone or cup?" Here is a country where its strawberry pickers speak several languages; English, Swedish, German, French, some Spanish and some Konkani, but some dentists only and only speak Finnish! At the same time here is a country where some young people with MA degree without any teaching experience teach some technical courses at university to MA and PhD students while some Finnish and non-Finnish people with PhD in hand and some years of postdoc fellowship in the same department are on unemployment benefit! This reminds me of a story: Once The Police Wo-Man perceives that in highway a cyclist is as fast as a new Mercedes Benz. The Police Wo-Man becomes curious and chases them to find how a bike can be so fast. Is the cyclist an Olympic gold medalist or what? When The Police Wo-Man approaches the Mercedes Benz and the bike, s|he finds that the cyclist has tightly held the right side view mirror of the Mercedes Benz.

The Police Wo-Man
Right. It was so funi. When did I narate tis to you? In sauna?

The Emigrant
Yes.

Since I had moved to another university, I had to move my office, too. I got a desk in a research hall shared by some other PhD candidates. Some of my colleagues in that research hall were are extremely nice, caring and helpful. This gives you energy when you have such type of people around. When some caring people are around, you feel comfortable. I just counted and remembered that I have changed office seven times due to renovation, scathing verbal, short hours of work, university change, etc. and seven symbolizes completion.

Finland has a nice tradition of karonkka, a type of formal post-doctoral party. I'm having mine tonight. I should have invited more than sixty people, more than sixty nice friends and colleagues but I should cut the number, since I could not afford it. So I went for half of them. I take the opportunity to apologize sincerely from my lovely friends who were not invited and appreciate their sense of understanding. Very impressive celebra-

136

tion it was will be become; nice food, nice restaurant, nice programs and nice speeches presented by nice professors, colleagues and friends will make made it a memorable event. I talked talk first based on tradition. I had have to tell everyone how much I appreciated appreciate their at10tion and affection. Lots of memories I mentioned in my speech and a lot more I had to omit; otherwise, I had have to talk for about two hours. Since the party is held in honor of my opponent, he was the second who gives gave his speech. My supervisors then delivered deliver their lovely speeches. Then lots of my colleagues, instructors and friends give gave will give marvelous speeches about our relationship. Very impressive! I'm proud of myself for having such lovely friends. These speeches are were accompanied by two pieces of music and a funny program devised by my colleagues in my department. I wish wished time had been frozen. There was only one thing lacking, our parents and siblings. I dreamed dreamt they were here to celebrate the night that has been their dream to see as well. I have another dream! I have another *dream*! I have another *dream*! I have a *dream* today!

I had my defense session and karonkka a few months ago. That was marvelous as well with the presence of my supervisors, opponent and my colleagues. Their presence and nice speeches made my party really warm and light in the cold dark winter. Like my husband I had a toastmaster. In fact my toast master and my husband's were both my colleagues who organized our parties. I am was very proud of my supervisors who helped me get my studies done in a marvelous way. I really appreciate their supports.

When I started, I was much younger and very much in love. I'm still in love. Many a lot changed in me during these years that I supposed will never change! This very day I can easily detect lots of gray hair amidst my dark brown locks. That signifies decay or what? I gazed at my faded youth. Now that my task has been achieved, am I immortal? My heart says you penned many pages, you left your name behind and you wouldn't die. I have learned that what we plant now we harvest later! What we give now we receive later, since for every action there is a reaction!

It's now time to take my daughter to music club. She practices flute under the supervision of a nice friendly Finnish teacher with a great worldview. I really enjoy interacting with him once a week and during my daughter's course. Right after coming back, I write about my pre-examiners' reports.

They are both positive and recommended that I be granted permission to defend my dissertation at a public examination! Hurray but it's not that simple and quick! Each of them has proposed some comments that I need to apply, introduced some books and papers that I have to find and buy, read and use in my work. Thus revision process would be time-consuming. I should start as soon as possible.

Is *No Place to Be Somebody* a comedy or a tragedy in you' opinion?

In his Poetics, Aristotle mentions that comedians who were excluded and banished from town wandered from village to village. Now that those values have been toppled, comedians are back to town. Let me add that the traditional firm generic divisions of comedy and tragedy have been blurred, thus it can be said that comedy makes one *think*, while tragedy makes one *feel*. Consequently, if reading and watching this play makes you feel, it's in fact a tragedy and if it makes you think it's a comedy. Based on this definition, this play might be a comedy for an audience and a tragedy at the same time for another audience sitting next to her|him.

I'm done! I applied some of the comments but one of them is a matter of style and I decided not to apply it. It says that the structure of my Introduction is "patchy!" But I would like to use "clear" instead of patchy to describe the structure of my Introduction. In fact, during my doctoral studies I read several dissertations in my field of research written and defended in different parts of the world, including Finland. Some of them had mixed up everything together with few subchapters in their introductions, while some others had classified their discussions under several subchapters. I found that the latter is more reader-friendly, since a glance is sufficient to direct readers to wherever they wish without needing to read the whole chapter if they do not want to. I liken these two different styles to two different cuisines. In the first cuisine, all ingredients are mixed together, chopped and then cooked, and after the food is ready it is difficult for diners to distinguish the used ingredients, whereas in the second cuisine each ingredient is cooked at a time, and then they are designed on plate so diners know clearly what they eat. In my meeting with my supervisors, we discussed this comment and we found it a matter of form and style rather than content. As for content, I should note that my introduction contains every necessary part that it must include such as the introduction of subject, the elaboration of my research questions, aims and methods, a review of literature and scholarships on Charles Gordone, the definition of my central concepts and the clarification of the novelty of my work in an elaborate manner. In his statement, the opponent confirms that the research problems are clearly explained in the Introduction and that the research questions and aims are well-presented. He also confirms that the thesis shows a good knowledge of previous research on Gordone. Based on this argument, I claim that my Introduction does not lack any necessary element but the way the discussions have been presented is a matter of subjectivity. I hope this does not affect my grade!

My supervisors double checked the work and revisions. Plagiarism checking is obligatory and then language checking. They take about 10 days, I reckon. Can you wait for more 10 days?

Let me checkmark them as well. I had to pay for language checking first and then ask for reimbursement from our Faculty. So I did file an application for language checking reimbursement. Everything seems complete. I need to wait for our dean's decision and permission. Thankfully, it is positive and I can proceed. Now I have to rush to our library, since I must sign a publication contract with them to receive publication grant. Its staff informed me in his email that he is heading for a tour round Europe by train and if I don't catch him today, he won't be available for about 10 days! What? 10 again? It's really writ10 in my destiny. I was amazed when I visited his office and found him with a weird cap on! He told that he has bought it during his visit to Indonesia. He was is a fan of adventure to unknown lands! He recounted some of his adventures and I really enjoyed lis10ing to him. Now it's time to sign the contract. Just there I found that I have to follow their cover design format and color which is not my favorite. He kindly advised me that there is one way to skip it and that is to use a cover image of my own. But how is it possible in this short period of time? Almost every image needs a copyright. Desperate!

I went to a publication house. I chose the one that published my wife's dissertation. Its staff responsible for layout and cover design is cool and patient as you are. He goes through your entire comments one after the other as if this is his own dissertation. I negotiated with him over the cover design problem. Like me, he

141

also thinks thought the cover format suggested by my Faculty is just ugly! "I have a suggestion for you," he said. "What?" "Just go to this website, find any image that you wish and I'll buy it for you in 10 minutes and do the formatting as well!" "Great news!" But will I find something suitable for my work in this website? Quickly I went back to my office and searched for some hours non-stop. I found some images which go went quite well with my subject but I chose a theater hall in blue. Why blue? That's a good question, because even if I choose an image for the front cover, I still have to take the blue color format determined by our Faculty for the back cover and spine. So the colors used in front cover should go together quite well with the colors of spine and back cover.

He kindly designed the cover. He had also sent the cover design for the library staff's approval. He was traveling and he confirmed it after he was back. The only problem with the cover design was that the title of the dissertation and my name had appeared on right alignment and I wanted it to appear right in center.

The Finnish Finn
I love center too. I'm tired of [isolation] and   remoteness.

The First Woman Voter
You know what? I hate centeredness.

But to be in center could not be done without the library staff's permission so I waited for him to come back from his trip. Then I

142

visited his office and negotiated with him. At first, he said that this cannot be done, but after I explained everything he kindly agreed. So I went back to the publication house and asked its staff to move the title to center and send the new design to our library for final approval. Done in a couple of days. I received the layout and I had to read it through to detect any possible mistake. I found some petty mistakes and the publication house staff removed them and gave me another layout! What could be better than that? This time my supervisor took care of that. He carefully read it through and with his keen observation he found a couple of mistakes. Done! The staff of the publication house then told me that I have to pay for the publication fee and then apply for refund from my Faculty. He said that they charge other faculties directly but my Faculty is an exception! Just about 10 minutes ago, he notified me that the books and karonkka invitation cards are were ready. I paid and then filed an application for refund. I receive the refunds shortly after but don't know what will happen with the tax office by the end of the year!

I had to distribute some copies of my dissertation to different offices of university and hand in some copies to my colleagues, professors and friends. Done in a few days. Then I learned from my supervisor that I have to book a lecture hall. I contacted staff responsible for it. She introduced several halls to me and I needed to visit them all to see which one suits me the most. Some were engaged when I reached there, so I had to wait till the classes or exams were over. Some were far, some were either tiny or huge! I found the best possible one near my department and later I found that I have been a type of Columbus or rather Before Columbus since many of my colleagues told me that this is was the first time that they have had been to that nice lecture hall. I had to go and thank that lady who responsibly and patiently helped me book such a marvelous place and I did. You can't imagine how happy she got when I went to her office in person and thanked her. It was as if you had given her the whole entire world! I was happy to see her happiness as well. Why some people are so responsible and some others are not?! Why some people are really nice but some others are ice? Why we wish to see some people every day while we hope NOT to bump into some others? Why meeting some people makes our day while meeting some others totally ruins it? This is nice to tell people about their commitment and sense of responsibility. I am confident that our appreciation shows that we understand their commitment, and this would encourage them to expand it.

Then I had to fill in the defense session announcement form and contact the university communication and public relations office to help them prepare the defense session news for their website and a local newspaper. Reception after the defense session is a tradition in Finland as well. My husband and I visited different places and after some negotiations, we finally signed a contract with a company to take care of it: coffee and chocolate cake.

Would you like to have some ccc now? If not, pleaase take a deep breath!

My car went out of order. I have lots of tragic stories with mechanics in Finland more than my stories with dentists. I have already lost a car. It had electrical problems and they couldn't find its problem and after charging me a couple of hundred euros for doing nothing sent me to its central coast. The car was there for about 10 days, and they said that they need a couple of thousand euros to shoot the trouble and when I refused to pay that amount, they charged me a couple of hundred euros for my refusal! Then desperately I sold the car to a dealer for a couple of hundred euros. Now the engine management light of this one is on. The local mechanic failed to find its problem and charged me for his failure and now the car is in its central coast. I am waiting for them to call and tell me how many thousand euros it costs!

Since I didn't impose any publication or language checking costs on our department, our head of department kindly accepted to cover half of the reception costs but I needed to pay it first and then file another application for refund. Karonkka and finding a nice restaurant was also a demanding job. My husband and I visited more than 10 restaurants, saw their facilities, negotiated with them and finally decided to sign a contract with the best possible choice. Sending out the invitation, programming, finding a toastmaster, checking the lecture hall and its equipment with my supervisor and a lot of small businesses were also a part of my

145

work. In the meantime I had to prepare my lectio that you lis10ed to at the beginning of this noveramatry. By the way, do you know that the end is in the beginning?

Now after five years that we finnished our studies and got our degrees we are indeterminate just like the time we wanted to leave our home country. We don't know whereto we belong? Here or there? We really don't know what to do now: to stay or to go? —.— By now our daughter is bright here at school but since she cannot write and read her mother tongue she might get educational blight after our return and this makes us worried. I should reread this poem now:

Indeterminacy

Indeterminacy kills us
Curiosity kills the cats
But wee've been born to die
As ephemeral arts do!
Any way not to die?
Confusion kills us
Double voicedness in head, two
Two or too?
You speak while silent
Your silence is heavy and light
Your speech smooth and harsh
I hesitant, you confused

Perhaps wee stay alive

if you stop and give me five

A hi five

You sure five is are enuf?

Which one? Is or are?

Are you sure?

Shall wee go?

Shall wee no?

Wee'll die if we're sure

But what four?

Four or for?

Incredulity kills us

Curiosity kills the rats

Confusion keeps us killed

Indeterminacy kills all!

Thankfully, my mechanic called me a couple of minutes ago and said that they have managed to find and shoot the trouble. There was something wrong with one of the injection valves so I have to go, pay its fees and get it back. I'll be back soon.

Onko minulla edes vähän aikaa tarkastella muistiinpanojani ennen väitöstilaisuutta? EI TODELLAKAAN! Vain pari päivää jäljellä ja minulla on vielä hirveästi tekemistä kuten tapaamisia ohjaajani ja seremoniamestarin kanssa sekä parin kaverin kanssa, jotka ystävällisesti lupasivat auttaa minua joissakin järjestelytehtävissä. Lisäksi minun pitää käydä ravintolassa

147

varmistamassa vieraitteni nimet ja heidän allergiansa. Sitten pitää vielä lähettää sähköpostiviestejä joillekin yliopistohenkilökunnan jäsenille ja käydä parturissa. . . .[39]

Oh, the opponent is standing so it seems that I have to stand up and lis10 at10tively to his final report. That's really important.

The Emigrant
The Finnish Finn
The Swedish Finn
The First Woman Voter
The First Finnish Immigrant
The Veteran
The Police Wo-Man
The Finnish Refugee
The Gabe Gabriel
King Charles Frederick

I am happy to be able to propose to the Faculty of Humanities that this disse'tation, entitled *Raceless Drama: A Study of Selected Plays by Cha'les Go'done* be accepted as a doctoral disse'tation.

Oh my God, I'm done! One of my dreams was interpreted but I still have a *dream*! I have a *dream* today! Five years were was compressed accelerated halted slowed down repeated revised stretched in two and half hours and 148 pages, so quick! I have no language to express my high excitement. I am near tears. THANK YOU FINLAND!

This disputation is now concluded.[40]

Endnotes

---

[1] It was very slippery.

[2] I myself didn't get anything. Sorry!

[3] I found that Finnish language is not that hard, and if you at10d Finnish language courses 24/7 for about only five years, you can surely acquire and speak it like a robot.

[4] How is it going?

[5] Please do some research on the notion of "sisu" if you wish.

[6] Magistrate office

[7] Do you remember that

[8] I speak a lot.

[9] The repetition of figments' names, followed by no dialogues, monologues or stage directions, may have many different significations. Readers and performers can participate and fill in the gaps in any way they wish. You can even write dialogues, monologues or stage directions for them.

[10] Really? What for?

[11] Silence is golden.

[12] Well-known

[13] What is well-known in English?

[14] Readers and performers should decide on speakers in case of hyphens.

[15] Thanks, yes.

[16] Nice to meet you.

[17] e. e. cummings

[18] [My translation]: Right! Write to live and live to write. As Faulkner says, "If a story is in you, it has got to come out."

[19] [My translation]: Don't be a waiter, but a writer. Start right now. Writing is fighting. And remember my maxim: no one has been born a writer, one becomes.

[20] [My translation]: I'm writing! Wait a tick, please.

[21] See you soon.

[22] Vihapuhe or "Hate speech" is defined as speech that attacks a person or group of people on the basis of attributes or behaviors related to their gender, ethnic origin, religion, race, disability or sexual orientation.

[23] I myself didn't get anything.

[24] Thanks a lot.

[25] What?

[26] Do you understand?

[27] Just wanted to bring you here to thank you for the time and energy you spend on reading my noveramatry.

[28] Are you a police officer?

[29] Yes

[30] After calling a detective two times and she did not answer her phone, I left her a voice message. I did not have her email address at all! This is exactly the same text message that her colleague sent to me on her behalf. I copied and pasted it and just . . . the names of the detective and her colleague.

[31] Triangular cotton scarf

[32] Just a moment.

[33] Summer cottage is more important.

[34] Bad feelings we had have!

[35] Iranian poet Saadi Shirazi wrote this poem eight centuries ago. The poem now graces the entrance to the Hall of Nations of the United Nations building in New York as an inscription:

بنی‌آدم اعضای یک پیکرند   که در آفرینش ز یک گوهرند

چو عضوی به درد آورد روزگار   دگر عضوها را نماند قرار

تو کز محنت دیگران بی‌غمی   نشاید که نامت نهند آدمی

[36] We replied Finland. He said, "I've heard that Finland is very finntastic. Its neighboring countries such as Singapore, Indonesia and Malesia are finntastic as well." And we surprisingly said, "What? Singapore, Indonesia and Malesia?! But Finland is in North Europe!" With his great knowledge of geography, we were happy that he did not take us to grave yard instead of airport.

[37] To me the main reason of divorce is "marri-age."

[38] Two ice-creams.

[39] Any time to study and review my notes before my defense? NO WAY! Only a couple of days left and I have lots of works, a meeting with my supervisors, a meeting with my toastmaster, a meeting with a couple of my friends who kindly promised to help me in a couple of administrative works, a visit to restaurant with my guests' names and their allergies, some emails to different staffs at university, a haircut. . . .

[40] Dear reader, I wish to thank you for your participation in re-writing this work.

Works Sighted

Booth, Michael. 2015. *The Almost Nearly Perfect People: Behind the Myth of the Scandinavian Utopia*. London: Vintage Books.

Bowie, Ian. 2013. *Simply Suomi*. Turenki: Kirjapaino Jaarli Oy.

Dahlgren, Maija and Marja Nurmelin. 2007. *Sauna, Sisu & Sibelius*. Helsinki: Yrityskirjat Oy.

Ellison, Ralph. 1952. *Invisible Man*. New York: Random House.

Kostiainen, Auvo, ed. 1990. *Finnish Identity in America*. Turku: Kirjapaino Grafia Oy.

Lee, Dorothy. 1976. "Three Black Plays: Alienation and Paths to Recovery." *Modern Drama* Vol. 19, No. 4, pp. 397-404.

Schwarzmann, Phil. 2011. *How to Marry a Finnish Girl:Everything You Want to Know About Finland That Finns Won't Tell You*. Helsinki: Gummerus Publishers.